Changeling Press, LLC

ChangelingPress.com

Utopia

Gale Stanley

Utopia
Gale Stanley

ISBN: 978-1-60521-855-7

Publisher:
Changeling Press LLC
315 N. Centre St.
Martinsburg, WV 25404
ChangelingPress.com

Printed in the U.S.A.

Editor: Kira Stone
Cover Artist: Bryan Keller

The individual stories in this anthology have been previously released in E-Book format.

Table of Contents

The Alpha's Demiwolf (Utopia 1)
Gale Stanley

Kya: I'm a demiwolf -- half wolf, half human -- and both species despise my weird mix of genes. Despite the fact I strip for a living, I've hung on to my virginity for twenty-two years. Until I got knocked up by a big, bad wolf. Now, I'm going to bring another demiwolf into the world, but his father will never know.

Levi: I'm all wolf, and Alpha of my pack, committed to keeping our bloodlines pure. Then on the night of my bachelor party, I hooked up with a stripper. I just wanted to teach the demiwolf a lesson, but the sex set me on fire. My wolf claimed her and now I can't get her out of my head. But what if she can't accept me?

Chapter One

Levi

By the time we hit the last club on our bar crawl, I was hungry for action. So far, the talent had been underwhelming, but now my expectations soared. Show 'n Tails had never failed to impress me before. It's no gentleman's club, just a down-at-the-heels titty bar, but it has the most athletic pole dancers I've ever seen. The club is open 24/7 and the management didn't discriminate. As long as a customer had deep pockets, they didn't care if he was a testosterone-fueled wolf-shifter who wanted to finger the merchandise or bust a few tables.

I had high hopes that my bachelor party would end with excessive fucking. Not that it mattered. This wasn't one last fuck before the wedding. In my world, screwing around doesn't end with marriage. The same doesn't hold true for she-wolves. Our women are held to a different standard. Enforced monogamy is the rule, and for good reasons. She-wolves are in short supply and we strive to keep our bloodlines pure. Yes, we're possessive hypocrites. It's not fair but that's the way it is.

The limo deposited us at the front door. Samson, my beta and best man, handed some cash to the bleary-eyed bouncer and we stumbled inside. The bright spotlights, loud music, and pungent aroma of human pheromones sent me into sensory overload, but it was all good. The place had sentimental value and being there brought back personal memories.

My father took me to Show 'n Tails when I was a cub and he was pack Alpha. My mother knew, but she turned the other cheek. Learning about sex from a hooker or a stripper has always been an accepted part of a male's education for wolf-shifters. In fact, it's compulsory for Alphas and I was well educated. The old man took me back many times. He doesn't fuck around anymore, but I still like to come back with my boys.

A little blonde wearing bikini bottoms and nothing else showed us to a table for four. She leaned over and shoved her rack in my face. "I'm on next."

"I'll be watching." I stuck my tongue out and licked her nipple. She giggled and turned away.

We ordered a round of drinks and Samson held up his glass. "To Levi." He looked from Milo to Axel. "You guys don't have a clue how fucking long I've waited to hear him admit that I'm the best man."

We all laughed, and Axel responded with his own toast. "To the kisses we've snatched and the snatches we've kissed."

Milo, never one to be outdone spoke up. "To our wives and girlfriends, may they never meet."

"I'll drink to that." I lifted my glass and downed half the contents.

The guys were only half joking. When the old man turned the reins over to me, he reminded me that I had a fiancée simmering on the back burner and it was time to marry. "You can still have fun," he said. "Keep a human girl or two on the side, but make sure she knows she's a side piece. No strings, just fucking."

It's well known that wolves have big sex drives. She-wolves are off-limits until marriage, but anything goes with human females. I knew from personal experience that the strippers at Show 'n Tails were ready, willing, able, and smart enough to protect themselves from accidents. The last thing I wanted to do was produce a half-breed. I just wanted a good time and the girls just wanted to make money. Of course, I'd make sure they enjoyed themselves, too. It was a win-win situation.

* * *

Kya

I cringed when I saw the billboard proclaiming, *Girls! Girls! Girls!* It was a tacky way to get attention, and I hated it. Averting my eyes, I turned the corner, pulled into the lot, and parked my old pickup behind the club. It was my first night at Show 'n Tails, and a definite step down from my old job, but I'd been fired and needed a gig ASAP. The incident wasn't my fault. There were two of us on the stage and Brandi was so sloshed she invaded my space and fell on her ass. As if that wasn't enough, she accused me of tripping her. Well, one thing led to another and we both got canned. Another girl told me that Show 'n Tails was hiring and I went for an audition. The manager was an asshat, but he doesn't ask too many questions. I like to keep a low profile.

This isn't the life I wanted, but taking off my clothes pays the bills, and I won't apologize for trying to earn a living. At least I'm not selling my body, just the illusion of sex. A lot of girls up their game, but not me. My virginity is the last piece of self-respect I own and I won't give it up to some creep for any amount of money.

The heavy backdoor slammed shut and locked behind me and the manager shot me a dirty look. "Hey, Kya. You're late."

"Sorry, it won't happen again. And my name is Raven when I'm working."

Marty's lip curled in a sneer. "Yeah, yeah. Whatever. You better get dressed. I mean undressed." He snickered.

I ignored his disrespectful ass, and walked over to the dressing room. A row of dented lockers lined one wall. A wide counter with a lighted mirror behind it ran the length of the opposite wall. Everything stunk from sweat and cheap perfume. The long vanity was cluttered with makeup and no one made room for the new girl, so I started changing next to my locker. When a spot at the mirror opened up, I grabbed it and started working on my wild black curls.

Marty stuck his head in the door. "Hey, fresh meat, you're on next."

I knew he meant me. I was the newest girl there. Half of me cringed, the half that's wolf. The half I keep hidden. Or is it a quarter of me I keep hidden? I guess it depends on how you look at it. A full-blooded wolf-shifter is already half human, although they'll never admit to it. My father was a wolf, but my mother was human. Does that mean I'm... Oh, fuck the fractions. No matter how you look at it, I'm a demiwolf.

But I look human. I checked my body in the mirror. Yep, a hot as hell human female stared back at me. Tacky, but sexy. Nothing says stripper like stiletto platform heels and a thong that shows off a girl's booty. I slipped on a white, halter mini-dress with a drape-neck, an open back, and a side slit. Then I ran my hands through my curls and gave my lips one last swipe of purple-plum gloss.

It's so much easier to call myself human and blend in with the majority. The humans are clueless. They know we exist, but they believe we keep to our own side of the tracks. The wolves are a different story. They can smell my lupine pheromones, but they don't want me. I'm not pure. Fuck 'em. At least I can make a living among the humans. Stripping might be a trashy job, but it pays for the life I'm trying to live. It's not the life I want, but it's all I've got. I used to dream about being accepted by my father's people. Fat chance. They wouldn't even accept him because he had a human lover and a half-breed kid.

My parents never married, but they lived together -- sometimes. When my father was around, I was daddy's girl. But all too often, he would disappear as if he had no family. My mother would drink and tell me that he liked to hang out with his own kind in places where we weren't accepted. When he came back from his trips, he'd act cold and resentful, but it wouldn't last long. Eventually, he'd tell me he loved me and everything would be okay again. I thought nothing would keep us apart for good. I was wrong.

One day he didn't come back. We found out he was killed in a bar fight. One of his so-called friends called me a mongrel and Dad died defending me. My mother cried and cried. She said this was why they never wanted kids. So I was what... an accident?

I couldn't blame them. Not really. Life was hard enough without being born with this weird mix of genes. I hated myself, too. I wished I'd never been born. At least I could make things easier for my mother. As soon as I finished school, I left home and never looked back.

While waiting to go on, I thought about my routine -- floor work, then pole dancing, then back on the floor. I'm not nervous anymore about being naked in front of a roomful of men. I was at first, but now I focus on my moves. I've been scorned and dehumanized all my life, so I like to emphasize something I can do well -- dance.

I peeked through the curtain and watched Candy finish her routine. There's a mirror behind the stage and a pole in the center. Chairs surrounded the stage for customers who wanted direct contact with the dancers. I watched one of the men put a bill in his mouth. Candy shoved her breasts in his face and used them to grab the money. There were hoots and hollers and more men waved bills at her. She collected all of her tips, then picked up her clothes, and ran off the stage.

The DJ, sitting in an alcove nearby, introduced me. "Next up is a beautiful lady who's new here. You're gonna see her naked for the first time tonight."

Well, it's not a complete lie. It's my first time naked on this stage.

"Give Raven a nice warm welcome."

My heartbeat skyrocketed as I stepped through the curtains and climbed the three steps to the stage. The opening bars of my music started up and I began to move.

* * *

Levi

My anticipation ran high. I'm always excited to see new talent. Samson made a joke about the taste of fresh meat and we all laughed, then I looked up at the stage and my eyes practically popped out of my head, like in one of those old cartoons. The new girl... what's her name? Raven. She took my breath away. Her curvy shape and that thick black mane had me salivating. From what I could see, everything looked natural, and she had the best set of legs in the club.

"That is one hot piece of ass." Samson stood up. "I need a closer look."

Samson walked over to the stage and we all followed. Raven smiled in our direction and my heart took a leap. Her white mini dress emphasized all that golden skin, but it was her eyes that really stood out.

Almond in shape and color, they seemed to be staring directly at me.

* * *

Kya

There was movement when I walked out. Evidently, the customers wanted a closer look at the fresh meat. Four men moved from their table to sit at the stage. I smiled at them because it's rule number one. Be nice to the customers, and it will pay off in more tips.

The tallest of the group locked his dark chocolate eyes on mine, and it was hot as hell. He was enormous with big, broad shoulders and masculine appeal. Thick brown hair framed a strong jaw with just the right amount of sexy stubble. One of his friends slapped him on the back. "Hey, Levi. She just eye fucked the shit out of you."

Levi winked and flashed me a cocky grin as his gaze raked my body. I felt my heart beat in my pussy and I knew I'd be dancing for him tonight.

What the fuck? That notion didn't come from me. Just like always, I chalked it up to wolf genes.

Growing up, I was a confused kid, reclusive and lonely. My only friend was a voice in my head that I called Raven. My mother called her an imaginary friend. She said Raven would disappear when I got older and learned to cope with life's problems.

But my father would bark at her in an angry voice. "You don't understand. Leave the girl be. Raven is her wolf spirit." He'd turn to me and explain. "Raven embodies your strong lupine traits. Embrace her and she'll protect you."

I didn't understand either, but my father must have been right, because Raven never went away.

Unlike me, she's aggressive and predatory, and doesn't mind taking her clothes off for strangers.

When I was younger, she scared the hell out of me. I worked hard to block out her voice, but my alter ego had a mind of her own and I was a dumb kid who didn't know how to control her.

Wolf-shifters are a minority. They live in their own neighborhoods and have their own schools. They didn't accept me or my mother, so we lived in a shitty apartment, and I went to a human school and tried to blend in. It worked until high school, and then everything changed.

Shy and quiet, I put up with a lot of bullying. I ignored it as best I could, but inside Raven's rage grew strong.

One day, the most popular boy in the school sat with me in the lunchroom. "Are you going to the dance Friday, Kya?"

I was speechless. I didn't think he even knew my name.

"Cat got your tongue?"

I looked down and shook my head. "I'm not going."

"That's too bad. I bet you'd look really pretty with a new dress and some makeup."

Suddenly, his friends were joining us at the table. Alarm bells went off and I made a move to get up.

The jock put a hand on my bare knee. "Don't leave. We're just getting acquainted." He slid his hand up my thigh and under my panties.

Did he think I wanted his attention that bad? I saw red and leaped up. Any barriers between Raven and myself crumbled. I crouched backwards as if ready to pounce and curled my lips to show my incisors. My hair stood on end as I let out an aggressive snarl.

The boys circled me. "You're one of those dirty animals, aren't you? Freak. Let's see your hairy body, wolf girl." One of the boys pulled at my skirt.

Without thinking, I sank my teeth in the meaty part of his hand, and he wailed like a banshee. Another boy yelled, "Oh my God, she bit you. Now you're a werewolf, too."

I let out a crazy sound, half laugh, half howl. Stupid kids. It doesn't work like that. It's all in the genes. But it brought me back to myself. I released the boy and stood there, horrified by my own behavior. The truth was, I couldn't have stopped myself. I had no control over my own actions. I was an observer like everyone else.

The authorities ignored the fact that I was assaulted. They kicked me out of school and I finished my education at an alternative school for losers like me. I kept a tight rein on Raven and stuck it out until I earned a diploma. Then I left home.

Through the years, I'd learned how to restrain Raven, but now I found myself losing control again. I'd never dealt with a sexually aroused Raven before, and her flirtatious feelings were overwhelming. I had to force myself to turn my back to the men and start my routine.

Putting all that pent-up sexual energy into my movements, I touched my toes. My mini dress rode high, and revealed my ass. It was a move I'd done many times, but tonight it felt especially provocative and exciting because I knew Levi was watching.

I straightened up, grabbed the pole with one hand, and undulated to the music. Pretending it was Levi, I straddled the pole between my legs and started grinding against it. I arched my back, letting my long black hair swing behind me, and rolled my hips to the beat. Was Levi enjoying the show?

I told myself it didn't matter. Putting the thought out of my head, I gripped the pole and wrapped a leg around it. One nimble move and I was upside down. I swung around the pole and then I flipped off, ending up in a split on the floor.

Lost in the music, I forgot about Levi as I transitioned from one fancy pole dance trick to another. An intricate, busy routine kept my mind occupied. I was always thinking of my next move, and not who was watching me.

The routine ended with a squat on the stage floor. Leaning against the pole, I brought my knees together and slowly slid back up. The men cheered me on and waved dollar bills in the air, but I only had eyes for Levi. I tore my gaze from his. It was time for the finale.

Visualizing myself as a beautiful snake, I made sure my slides and splits flowed together with grace and emotion. I smiled, gripped the hem of my dress, pulled it over my head, and tossed it aside, revealing the thong and bikini top I wore underneath. Hips swaying, I tossed my hair and unhooked the bra. It was strapless and it fell to the floor. Levi and his machismo-fueled posse howled like a bunch of frat brothers. I didn't mind. When I'm dancing, I forget the hostile world I come from and I pretend the compliments and catcalls are genuine. It gives me an ego boost.

My breasts are big and natural, and they bounced as I strutted around the stage in my G-string. I've danced naked too many times to count and I'm usually comfortable in my own skin, but this time I was all too aware of my body and the handsome stranger watching me. I kept glancing over at him. He was staring at me intently and the air seemed to buzz between us.

More men moved from the bar to the stage and shouts of, "take it all off," filled my ears. The men looked at me as if I were a lamb surrounded by wolves. Little did they know that I was the beast, and they were the frail lambs.

The chants got louder and I gave the customers what they wanted. I slipped off my G-string, surprised by how damp it was. Then I leaned against the pole, slid down into a sexy squat, and let my knees fall apart. All the men cheered, but I looked for Levi, teasing him with a perfect view of my wet pussy.

Fives and tens fluttered in the air and the pile of bills on the stage grew bigger. Levi called my name and held out a fifty-dollar bill. I didn't see those too often. A few more and maybe I could get my truck fixed. I let my body melt to the floor and crawled toward him. He watched with glittering eyes.

When I got close, I inhaled his spicy fragrance. *Wolf!* There was no mistaking his unique scent. Levi's eyes turned hard. *He smells me, too.* There was no hiding from him. Our scent glands produce pheromones, our own personal signature, and smell is the strongest of our senses. Despite my panic, one sniff boosted the arousal pulsing between my thighs. And I needed that money. Shaking, I grabbed for the bill, but he held it out of my reach.

"I'll give you this and more for a lap dance."

No way. I was afraid of what he'd say or do, but even more afraid of the animal lust consuming my body. I'd had the lecture from my father. "Be careful," he'd told me. "Your wolf DNA can get you into trouble. You're bound by your nature. If the right shifter appears, animal chemistry can draw you to him, like a moth to flame. Your arousal will consume you and it will be next to impossible to deny him sex."

I'd never felt such a pull before, but I knew this must be what he meant. This attraction was so strong, I wasn't sure I could fight it, but I intended to try. "I can't give you a lap dance."

His voice got louder. "Bullshit. Isn't that your job?"

I started stuttering. "I have to d-d-dance on the stage."

Marty appeared behind the boys. "Anything wrong here, fellas?"

The wolf waved the fifty under Marty's nose. "Raven says she can't give us a lap dance because she has to be on stage."

Marty grabbed the fifty and gave me a hard look. "Raven knows the customer always comes first. She'll meet you in the back. Last room on the left. Right, Raven?"

Inside I was seething, but I didn't want to lose my job. "Right. Soon as I finish here and change."

Marty left with his fifty. I scooped up the rest of the money. Then I slipped my dress on and looked for Marty. "I have to leave. I'm sick."

"It's your first fucking night. You just have the jitters."

"I'm sorry. It just came on."

"You don't look sick. These guys have money to burn. Bite the bullet, kid. If you leave, don't come back."

I couldn't afford to lose another job. And my damn pheromones pulled me toward the wolf. I headed for the changing room to get ready.

* * *

Levi

Samson took a deep sniff as Raven fled the stage. "I've never seen a she-wolf flaunting her body in public like that. You could get in trouble fucking her. We should take her back to the pack and question her."

I snarled. "She's not a she-wolf, she's a half-breed."

"You sure? How can you tell?"

"Damn it, Samson. Don't be stupid. Her pheromones are wrapped in human stink. She's perfectly fuckable."

Samson frowned. "I don't know. She's still part wolf."

"And she should take pride in that. I say we teach her a lesson."

I had to admit it was more about getting my hands on her than teaching her a lesson. When Raven's body was revealed in all its sleek splendor, I'd gone into a trance. When I looked into her eyes, I had tunnel vision. I didn't care what she was, I only knew I wanted her.

Chapter Two

Levi

My buddies followed me down a dim hall lined with booths. There were no doors, just bead curtains, and I could see plenty of activity going on behind them. My temperature ramped up another few degrees. The last booth on the left was empty. I sat in the chair and the boys stood. Where the fuck was Raven? I was impatient. I knew she wanted me, I could smell it all over her. And why not? I looked good. I'm not vain, just stating the facts. Six feet, six inches of hard muscle is tough to ignore. I wore a white button-down shirt with rolled up sleeves, and my tight jeans showed off a good-sized bulge. No jock or underwear on this wolf. Like most shifters, I went commando, less clothes to worry about when I shifted. Or scored a quick fuck.

But it was more than my big package that drew Raven to me. It had to be the wolf genes. Lupine DNA gives me a feral edge that attracts human women, but with another wolf, it can be magnetic. Raven wasn't a pureblood, but my pheromones still attracted her like a bee to honey. And vice versa.

Finding her here had been completely unexpected, and totally electrifying. I'd never fucked a she-wolf. Normally I had to control my urges around them, but tonight I would experience sex with one of my own kind. Well, not really my kind, but close enough. Making it more exciting was the fact that I was supposed to shun her. Not gonna happen. I've always been tempted by forbidden fruit and Raven was exquisite. Watching her perfect naked body moving around the stage had made me hot, horny, and anxious to get inside her.

* * *

Kya

I don't fuck. Not for money, not for anything. And no, I'm not waiting for *the one*. I don't harbor false expectations of finding the love of my life. I'm sure there are plenty of good reasons for being celibate, but the fact is, my virginity is the last untouched piece of me and I refuse to give it to some disrespectful jerk. The humans think I'm an animal and the wolves treat me like an aberration, a mistake of nature. Men have made me so much less than I might have been.

On the other hand, I knew Levi expected sex and I didn't know how to get out of it. At my last job, penetration was a no-no, but I was quickly learning that at Show 'n Tails, nothing was off limits as long as the customer had the cash. I just hoped his friends didn't want a piece of me too. Talking a bunch of wolves out of sex, especially after an erotic lap dance, would never work. They already had a low opinion of me. They'd never believe I was a twenty-something virgin.

The best-case scenario would be if I got sick, but I doubted if I could puke on cue. There had to be another way. Then it came to me. They wouldn't believe the truth, but maybe they would believe a lie. I'd tell them I had an STD and hope they'd settle for blowjobs. Levi would be angry for sure, but there wasn't a damn thing he could do about it.

The only flaw in my plan was Raven. She and Levi shared an overwhelming compulsion that drew them together. I wasn't sure I was strong enough to deny Levi something that my better half wanted so badly.

Marty stuck his head in the door of the dressing

room. "Get a move on, Raven. You have customers waiting."

I changed into a pink miniskirt, bra top, and matching heels, took a deep breath and made my way to the booth. The four big men inside didn't leave much room for me. I stood at the doorway, heart pounding, while they smiled and licked their lips. They were all good-looking, but Levi had all my attention. I couldn't take my eyes off him.

A throbbing started between my legs and my knees turned to jelly. My nipples went hard and goosebumps rose on my body. The few pieces of clothing I wore felt way too tight. I couldn't wait to strip them off. My plan was not off to a good start.

The music started and I shimmied, the beads accentuating my movements. Strutting past all that towering male flesh, I ended up in front of Levi.

One of the men slapped Levi on the back. "What do you think, Alpha?"

Alpha! I froze as a shot of adrenaline sent panic coursing through my body. I should have known he was an Alpha. Power and potency rolled off him in waves. Bad enough I was dancing for a bunch of wolves, this made it so much worse. The Alpha was the most powerful man in the pack. Even humans acknowledged that fact. Levi could get me fired, run me out of town, or even kill me, and no one would give a damn.

Levi looked straight at me. "I think she has too many clothes on."

"You heard the Alpha," his friend barked. "Speed it up."

Levi glared at his buddy and the man backed off. Reaching into his pocket, Levi pulled out a hundred dollar bill and held it up.

"Come on, Raven. Show me your pussy."

I wanted the money, but I was outnumbered and fear held me back. "It's too crowded in here."

Levi laughed aloud. "Oh, so that's it. You want more money." He pulled three more hundreds from his pocket. "Give us a good show and it's all yours."

Did he purposely misunderstand me? Probably. But four hundred dollars pays for a lot of humiliation. Despising myself, I reached for the money.

Levi held it out of my reach. "It's yours, after you dance." He shoved the bills back into his pocket.

I was pissed, but the money was a huge incentive and much as I hated to admit it, there was more than money spurring me on. I'd never been so aroused by a man. My stomach did flips as if a thousand butterflies had taken off inside me.

I slid my hands over my body, turned my back to him, and touched my toes. My skirt rode up, revealing my thong.

Levi slid his hand between my thighs and rubbed my slit under the G-string. He ignited a spark that inflamed my pussy and skittered down my legs. I froze.

"Hmm… You're so wet, Raven." He slid two fingers inside me. "Does this feel good?"

I couldn't hold back a moan.

"Yeah, you like it, slut." He removed his fingers and smacked my ass.

Reluctantly, I stood up and faced him. Watching him suck his fingers clean of my juices sent a shiver of anticipation down my spine, but I tried not to react as he teased me with his heated looks. His dark eyes were already undressing me and damn it, I wanted to be completely naked before him.

"Let me see you dance, Raven." Levi grabbed his

crotch. "I know you want it bad, and I'm gonna give it to you good, but first, I want to see you move that ass."

Now. Tell him now. I opened my mouth, the lie on my lips --

Levi reached out and cupped my chin tenderly in his warm hand. He caressed my cheek with his thumb. "So beautiful."

Then he leaned forward and his lips brushed mine, wiping away the lie, and everything else in my head. Shocked, I kissed him back. I'd never been kissed before, not like that, and I tried to pull away before I lost myself completely, but it was already too late. I could no longer think straight.

Levi trailed his lips down to my neck. Gently, he nipped and sucked at my sensitive flesh. *Oh, God. Is this how it feels when you make a real connection? Is this gentle man the real Levi? Or is it just wishful thinking?*

In my head, I knew a real connection was impossible, but Raven wanted him. Or was it me who wanted Levi's touch, his kisses, his cock? I didn't know anymore.

* * *

Levi

Raven's eyes went wide when I sucked my fingers. Her taste sent me reeling. Heat coiled in my belly and I wanted to howl at the moon. I was completely unprepared for the feelings that swept through me.

Without thinking, I cupped her face and kissed her. She kissed me back. Our breaths mingled. Fuck, did she have to be so damn perfect? She set me on fire. My breathing speeded up, so did hers. I started to nuzzle her neck and I felt her body tremble. Drunk on pheromones, I didn't want this to end. Her kiss was a promise of much more to come.

"Come on, Levi. Knock off the kissy, kissy. We want to see her dance."

I heard laughing all around me and I froze. Fuck, I'd forgotten we weren't alone. An Alpha doesn't kiss strippers or half-breeds. I pushed Raven away. "Okay, slut, do what you do best."

She cringed and a tear escaped one eye. My heart twisted. Then her expression turned hard, as if she were a different person. Turning her back to me, she swayed to the music, then unhooked her bra and threw it at Samson, making him gasp. "Now that's more like it."

She turned to face me. Her tits were full and firm. She cupped them, lifting them high, and twisting her caramel nipples between her fingers. My friends were salivating, rubbing their swollen dicks through their jeans. It bothered me and I didn't know why. We watched each other all the time, even shared. No sharing tonight. Raven was all mine.

Raven's movements hypnotized me as she took a few steps closer. Her eyes closed as she swayed with the music and traced the curves of her body. She played with the zipper on her skirt, pulling it up and down, tantalizing me. Coming closer still, her nose touched mine and I felt her warm breath. I almost stole a kiss, but she backed off too quickly. Her zipper went down one last time and the skirt fell to the floor. She kicked it away. I could see her slit through the material of her G-string. The triangle of fabric was soaked. Clearly, she was as hot as I was.

She slid the tiny patch of material down her legs, revealing her bare pussy, and threw the G-string at me. I raised it to my nose and took a deep sniff. Fuck! Pressure built deep inside me. I tamped it down, afraid

I was going to bust a nut in my jeans.

Loud groans sounded around me and from the corner of my eye, I saw the boys vigorously jerking off. I wanted to tell them to get lost, but before I could open my mouth, Raven put her hands on my knees and pushed my thighs apart. She sank between them and reached for my zipper. In an instant, my hard cock was freed and pointing at the ceiling.

"Now doesn't that feel better?" Her voice rolled over me like honey. Sultry, and slightly breathless, it made me swoon. I reached out to grip her hair --

She slipped from my grasp. Standing just far enough away so I couldn't touch her, she swayed her hips to the music and those beautiful tits jiggled in time to the beat. Her moves were smooth and erotic, teasing. She let me take in all that she had to offer, and it drove me crazy. Her smile was wicked, as if she knew exactly what she was doing to me and was enjoying every minute of it. Turning her back, she started twerking. I couldn't take my eyes off her shaking booty. An involuntary groan escaped my throat. Raven stood, looked over her shoulder and flashed me a sly smirk.

I didn't want her or the guys to know how she was affecting me, so I turned my groan into a growl.

"You stupid cunt. I'm paying for a lap dance. That means you on my lap."

Her eyes got all glassy. For a second, I thought she was going to cry. I softened at her stricken expression. *Why am I being such a prick?* I was about to tell her to forget it, but then her features contorted with anger. "That will cost you more."

I felt like an ass. The greedy bitch didn't deserve sympathy. She'd do anything for money. I flashed her a mocking grin. "Don't worry, you'll be well paid."

Raven didn't move.

"What? You don't trust me? Here's an advance." I peeled two hundreds off my roll and threw them at her.

She stared daggers at me. One minute, sweet and sad, the next, angry and vengeful. Did the bitch have a split personality?

Raven pushed the bills in the corner with her hooker heel. Nostrils flaring, she straddled my lap and clutched the back of the chair. Moving over me, she grazed my prick with her pussy. My eyes rolled back. Sucking in a deep breath, I palmed her breasts and massaged them until her nipples went stiff. She started making quiet whining sounds and rubbing her nose against mine. Knowing she was aroused electrified me. I was way beyond the point of control; I needed to be inside her.

* * *

Kya

I rubbed up against Levi and he let out a sound that was half groan, half growl. He held onto me, the two of us sniffing and licking wherever we could. Raven and I were hot and ready to fuck, but Raven preferred doggie style. I found myself wriggling off Levi's lap and turning my back.

Levi hoisted me up. His dick was poised at the wet folds of my pussy. I heard the men urging him on and I felt my face heat. I wanted to chase them out, but it wasn't my place. Despite my humiliation, I was completely turned on. A throbbing sensation pulsed in my vagina and I ached to be filled.

I was glad I had my back to Levi. I wanted him inside me, but I couldn't bear to look at his face while he fucked me. I needed to pretend that he really wanted *me*. Reaching down for his cock, I guided it to my dripping pussy and pushed down on him. We both drew in our breath at the same time.

As wet as I was, there was still pain. "Ow…"

Levi froze behind me. He whispered softly, for my ears only. "I know I'm big. You set the pace. I won't rush you."

He smelled like a strong wild animal, but he spoke so gently, I melted. I let out a breath and took it slow. When he was fully seated inside me, the pain disappeared and a euphoric feeling came over me.

"How does that feel now, Raven?"

All I could do was nod.

"Tell me."

I whimpered. "Feels good."

Levi groaned loudly. "Yes it does. You're so fucking tight. Ride me, Raven."

Shuddering, I began to slide slowly up and down on his shaft. Totally lost in animal heat, I was an unthinking ball of sensation. I forgot that three men were watching. It was just Levi and me. We were the only two people who mattered.

Levi reached around and pulled on my nipples. Every tug went straight to my pussy, and an orgasm built inside me. I started moving faster.

"Oh, yeah, that's it, baby." Levi kept up a steady stream of dirty talk. "I'm going to fuck your tight wet pussy until I blow my load inside you." He bucked his hips up, creating more friction. Then he rested a hand on my mound and started playing with my clit.

The walls of my pussy contracted around him and I let out a groan. "Oh, God." I felt like such a slut, such a whore, and I loved every minute of it.

Levi moved me up and down on his cock like a piston. Suddenly, he growled and sank his teeth into the tender flesh between my neck and shoulder. It hurt like hell, and I screamed.

Marty stuck his head in the booth. "What's going on here?"

The three wolves blocked his way, and one shoved some money into his hand.

"My mistake," Marty said. "Sorry I disturbed you." He turned his back and left.

Levi licked my wound, and the pain was replaced by more pleasure. Suddenly, he pulled me back, driving deep, deep, deep inside me. My pussy convulsed around his flesh as he filled me with load after load of hot cum. His climax triggered mine and I howled with ecstasy.

Savage animal sounds filled my ears and I realized they were coming from me. I was in a primal place, lost in the sensations bombarding me. Levi's hands roamed my body and the least little touch sent me into a flurry of spasms. I reveled in the feeling of him inside me, his touch, his smell…

Gradually, the sound of music broke through my delirium and I opened my eyes. Confused at first, I looked around. The three wolves were gone. I vaguely remembered Levi growling as he sent them away.

I was happy that Levi didn't want to share me. His cock was still hard inside me, and, lost in the afterglow of my orgasm, I squeezed my muscles around it, sending shivers of excitement through both of us.

Levi kissed the mark of his bite, then I felt him freeze. "Fuck," he blurted out. "What the fuck did I do?"

I giggled, and I haven't done that in years. "I believe you fucked me. In fact, you're still inside me."

He cursed under his breath. "This wasn't

supposed to happen."

I was baffled. Had he suddenly realized he'd defiled a wolf, and developed some scruples? "It's okay. I won't tell if you don't."

"It's not okay," he said bitterly. "And it's too late for secrets. My boys know."

"So what? They'll just give you a high five for making another conquest."

"More likely they'll mock me and criticize me for getting stuck with you."

"Stuck?" My temper flared. "This was your idea. You picked me."

"Yes, I did, and you're a great lay, but I never should have fucked you."

I swallowed a sob. Damn, why was I so emotional and teary-eyed? *What did you expect,* I asked myself. I should be long past expecting affection. I buried my emotions and hid behind Raven's hard shell. "Let me go, you big ape, and we'll forget it ever happened."

"Not gonna happen. Neither one of us is moving for the better part of an hour."

"What?" My body trembled, not with passion, but with white-hot fury. "You shouldn't have fucked me, but you want to do it again? I don't think so." I struggled to get off him, but I couldn't pry myself loose.

Levi let out a sarcastic laugh. "You're not going anywhere."

"Oh yes, I am."

"Oh no, you're not. Surely you know what's happening?"

"No. Tell me."

"I already did. We're stuck." He paused uncertainly, then slipped a finger along his dick inside my pussy. He held it up. It was covered with our fluids -- and blood. His voice was a strangled gurgle. "Is this your first time?"

"So what if it is?"

"Fuck! Why didn't you tell me?"

"Would you have believed me?"

"No." Levi was quiet for a moment. "This is your fault," he said scornfully. "You seduced me."

"You're crazy." My voice cracked with rage. "I did no such thing."

"Of course you did. It's your job." He swore under his breath. "You smile, shake your tits and your ass. You'll do anything to take our money."

"And you were willing to pay any price for my submission."

"Like I said, you seduced me. Besides, I wanted to teach you a lesson."

"You wanted to humiliate me."

"A she-wolf should have more respect for herself."

"But according to you, I'm not a she-wolf, just a half-breed."

"That's right. A she-wolf would have more pride. Our women wouldn't be caught dead showing their bodies to a bunch of strange men, let alone fucking one of them."

There was no way I'd tell the jerk how badly I needed this job, or how my pheromones left me no choice but to submit. "You seemed to enjoy yourself."

"Like I said, you're a good fuck, but I didn't expect..." He waved a hand around. "This."

"This?"

"Stop playing dumb." There was a sneer in his voice. "We're locked together for God knows how long. Your blood probably triggered my knot and the muscles in your vagina tightened around it. I can't pull out until I go soft."

Oh, my God. I'd heard of the wolf's knot, but I never thought I'd experience it, so I didn't pay much attention. I could feel it now, a bulb at the base of his penis, swollen and coated in our fluids. It was tying us together, and I was holding it firmly inside me. Still, I refused to take all the blame. "It takes two to tango."

"Why am I even bothering to talk to you?"

"Then don't." I wanted to cry. I'd lost my virginity to a creep who didn't deserve it and now I was impaled on his dick for another hour. The last shred of my dignity was gone, killed by my lust.

Lost in our own thoughts, neither one of us spoke after that. I started thinking with my head, instead of my vajaja. There was a reason for the knot and it had to do with reproduction. Oh, fuck. Levi hadn't used a condom, and being a committed virgin who didn't want to pump synthetic hormones into her body, I wasn't on the pill.

* * *

Levi

I can't believe this. How could I have been so stupid? Damn my animal lust. It took me completely off-guard. I shouldn't have been thinking with my dick, but this had never happened before, not with any woman, and I've been with plenty. My father always said that knotting would happen when I found my mate and lycan chemistry would tie us together so we could reproduce. Raven might have some lycan genes but she is most definitely not my mate. Why did she let me pop her cherry? The answer was obvious. She wanted a big pay-off. And she'd get one. At least I didn't have to worry about bringing another half-breed into the world. All the sluts who work here use protection.

After a while, I calmed down. Raven wasn't my mate, but she felt really good in my arms and her tight sheath around my dick made me think about round two. It wasn't fair to blame her for everything. I'd really wanted her, still did. She must hate me. I gave her a little nudge. "You okay?"

Raven's back went ramrod straight. "Now you ask?"

"Hey, you latched onto me, remember?"

"It's just like a man to blame the woman. You must have known this would happen."

"Well... uh, no. I didn't. It never happened before."

"How is that possible?"

"I never fucked a she-wolf before."

"And you didn't tonight. Your kind doesn't see me as a wolf, remember?"

I didn't answer. What could I say? My knot swelled, so obviously my wolf recognized her as another wolf.

She wasn't about to let up. "So you only fuck human women because they don't tie you down?"

"Yes, and she-wolves don't have sex until they're married."

"Nice," Raven said sarcastically. "So why pick me? Never mind, I get it. Number one, I'm not a real she-wolf and number two, I'm a stripper and a half-breed, so I must be a slut. I don't get a pedestal like your precious she-wolves."

It was true. Suddenly, I felt like a real jerk. I looked at me through her eyes and I saw a selfish bastard. I knew I'd hurt her feelings and I regretted it. I wanted to make it better. "It's not like that. You're not like the other…"

"Crossbreeds? Mutts? Freaks? Am I supposed to be flattered?"

"I wasn't gonna say that."

"Yes you were. At least admit it."

"Okay, I admit it. What can I say? I was raised to feel superior to humans and they're raised to feel superior to us. We think they're weak, and they think we're animals. Is it any wonder we don't want to mix our blood with theirs?"

My words hung in the air. After a longish pause, Raven replied. "I get it. My mother was human, my father a wolf. They were very different, but they loved each other, and I loved them. They were all I had. I had no friends. Then my father died and my world turned upside down."

"What happened to him?"

"He was killed by his own kind because he defended me. So, yes, I know all about prejudice. I don't trust either side, and it kills me that I have to pretend to be human just to get a job and exist." She broke off with a little cry. "I don't know why I'm telling you all this."

My heart ached for her suffering. I'd never known a demiwolf, just what I'd been told. What if everyone was wrong? Then I felt guilty for doubting my parents and the pack. "That's rough. I'm sorry you had to go through all that. It's why we abide by the laws of nature. Like attracts like."

"Birds of a feather flock together," she whispered.

"Yes." I hesitated, confused. "And yet I'm completely attracted to you."

Raven's voice was so low I could barely hear her. "I feel the same."

"Wanna have make up sex?"

My joke relieved the tension and we both laughed. Something life-changing had just happened, but I had no time to pursue it. My knot softened and Raven eased off me. I reached for her. "Hey, what's your real name?"

She considered my question, but before she could answer, Samson and the others showed up.

Shit, I was completely wrecked. "Your timing is impeccable," I muttered.

"Sorry, Levi. We gotta go. It's late and the driver needs to get the car back."

"Yeah, yeah." I managed to grab Raven's hand before she ran out, and I slipped all my cash into it.

She gave me a sad little smile before she ran out the door.

Chapter Three

Kya

I blamed Raven for what happened. I'd never let a man get to me like that before. I'd held onto my virginity for twenty-two years. Why had I given it up now? Was it because I knew marriage wasn't in my future? Prince Charming wasn't coming to sweep me off my feet. Raven had wanted to fuck, so why not enjoy one night of casual sex with no strings?

I still cursed myself for not trying harder, but the truth damned me. I couldn't say no. I was a slave to my wolf DNA. My body had betrayed me and I was powerless to resist the big, bad wolf. At least I'd enjoyed it.

I thought about how good it felt to have Levi's arms wrapped around me, his enormous cock inside me... Yes, I was being stupid. I knew the arrogant bastard wasn't spending his days pining over me, but a girl never forgets her first time. And Levi had left me a reminder that I would have for the rest of my life.

After a week went by, I knew I was in trouble. My period was late, and I'm never late. Then I started feeling queasy, and I never get sick. I finally gave in and bought a pregnancy test. The five-minute wait time after I peed on the stick was the longest of my life. I just knew it would come up positive. I wasn't even shocked when the two lines appeared. Instinctively, I put a hand on my stomach, already feeling protective of the new life inside me. But could I take care of a baby?

Practical questions raced through my mind. Soon I wouldn't be able to work, not with a big belly hanging over my G-string. I could find a different job. "Do you want fries with that?" But working fast food wouldn't support me and soon I'd have another mouth to feed. And who would watch the baby while I went to work? Daycare cost big bucks. And this apartment was barely big enough for me. The list of challenges went on and on and on.

Only one thing was certain. I would never give up my baby. My child might not have a father, but he or she would have a loving mother. Somehow, I would make it all work. Asking Levi for help was not an option. He'd fucked me the night of his bachelor party. He was probably already married, and for sure, he would not want to bring a demiwolf into the world.

If he knew about my pregnancy, he might pressure me into an abortion. Raven and I would never agree to that. I didn't believe Levi would hurt me or the baby, but I didn't trust his pack. What lengths might they go to, to prevent this birth? I had to get out of town. Fast. But where?

I hadn't seen my mother for several years. For all I knew she might have drunk herself to death, but I had no choice. I didn't tell anyone I was leaving, not even work. Packing went quickly. I didn't have much. Hoping the truck would make it to Philly, I headed home.

* * *

Levi

I live in upstate New York, in one of those small towns surrounding Adirondack Park. The park is one of the wildest areas in the East, and so isolated it's perfect for a wolf-shifter who wants to go for a four-footed run, or needs a peaceful place to think. I needed both. I slowed down and stopped by a small stream for a drink. Then I sprawled by the bank to get my head on straight.

Two weeks had passed since the night at Show 'n Tails, and I couldn't get Raven out of my head. Not a day went by that I didn't think about her. Sure, I wanted to fuck her again, but my thoughts went way beyond sex, and that was hard to understand.

I'd be working in my office, taking care of pack business, and out of the blue I'd feel a pull from her spirit that would set me worrying. Was somebody giving her trouble? Did she need me? For a while, I tried to ignore the whole thing, but my obsession with Raven became a constant distraction. I'd never had a connection that felt so deep.

I'd heard stories of magnetic energy and heightened awareness between mated pairs, but I always thought it was bullshit. Besides, Raven and I weren't mated and never would be. A connection with a demiwolf went against everything I've ever believed in.

Besides, I was about to marry Delilah, my real mate, and she demanded all my attention. Her family lived in the Midwest and we'd only met once before when my parents visited hers to arrange our marriage. She was a shy kid back then. Well, she wasn't shy anymore, and she wasn't the submissive mate I was expecting.

Delilah arrived with a sense of entitlement and a list of rules for me to live by. Her parents must have spoiled her and she expected me to do the same. She thought being the Alpha's wife empowered her. She even felt justified in telling me how to run the pack. Delilah actually told me to give my beta more responsibility because he was more diplomatic than I was.

The woman was driving me crazy, and not in a good way. We were on opposite sides of the spectrum about everything. What excited me, bored her, and she made sure to tell me. Every time we were together, my mood took a nosedive. Worse yet, I didn't feel any physical attraction to her. That was huge, but there was an even bigger deal breaker.

Delilah was new school, a she-wolf who believed what was good for the husband was also good for the wife. She demanded either a monogamous commitment or an open marriage for both of us. No way, either way. If my wife took a lover, I'd be the laughingstock of my pack, and if I couldn't take a lover, I'd be the laughingstock of my pack.

I was already on thin ice with my boys. After I'd knotted Raven and kicked my friends out of the booth, they called me pussy whipped. They couldn't believe I'd let a demiwolf lock onto me. To make it worse, it was the first time I hadn't shared with them. Samson wouldn't let it go. He called me a greedy bastard. Accused me of being afraid that he would steal my thunder. Ha! As if he could. I just kept telling him that I was enjoying myself too much, which was true. I couldn't tell him I had strong proprietary feelings for a demiwolf. Hell, I'd bitten the bitch. She was mine.

Being my boys, they promised to keep their mouths shut. What happened at Show 'n Tails stayed at Show 'n Tails, but if they found out I'd traded in my testicles and let Delilah put me on a short leash, I'd lose all respect. The pack respected me but if they sensed any weakness, I'd be forced to defend myself. Worst-case scenario, Samson could take my place. That would kill me for sure.

I needed to come up with a plan to handle Delilah. Our arrangement was not a love match. I knew we'd be miserable together, but our fate was sealed. Arranged marriages are arranged for the good of our species. It's all about economics and reproduction, and no one dares to object because our primary responsibility is to the pack.

The situation was driving me crazy. Somehow, I had to appease the pack, placate Delilah, and find a little joy for myself.

Inside my fur, I felt Raven pulling at me and I got an idea. My only option for some happiness was to keep Raven in my life. I had to see her and make sure she was okay, and while I was there, I'd offer her a proposition. I'd offer to set her up in an apartment and make her my girlfriend, a.k.a. my secret sidepiece. She would have a better life, and so would I. Delilah would never know.

* * *

Kya

I hadn't seen my mother in years, so I didn't expect a warm welcome, but she totally surprised me, wrapping me in a tight bear hug.

"Kya, baby, I'm so happy to see you."

It had been a long time since anyone had hugged me like that, and I snuggled into her arms as if I were five years old again. Finally, she released me and pulled me inside. I didn't smell any booze on her. Her apartment appeared clean and so did she.

"Where have you been? I missed you so much."

"I've been living in New York. I needed to get away, mama. You and daddy suffered enough because of me."

She looked horrified. "Nothing that happened was your fault."

My next words came out with a sob. "You said I was an accident. I thought you didn't want me."

"Damn my drunken mouth. I gave it up, baby.

Haven't touched a drop since you left." She embraced me again. "Oh, baby. You were an accident, but a happy one. Your father and I didn't want to bring a child into a world that wouldn't accept it, but when we found out I was pregnant, we felt blessed. You were always loved. I wish we could have done better for you."

Suddenly, we were both crying. Mama dried our tears with her apron and I followed her into the small kitchen that I remembered so well.

"Sit down," she said. "Are you hungry? Thirsty?"

"Can I have some water, please?"

Mama filled two glasses and set them on the table. We sat on opposite sides and sipped at the water.

"I was so worried about you, Kya. I looked everywhere. The police were no help. They thought you were a runaway."

I smiled. "I was, mama."

She smiled back. "Yes, I guess you were. I blame myself. If I hadn't been so drunk all the time…"

I reached across the table and put my hand over hers. "You were grieving."

"Yes, for your father and for you."

"I'm sorry I left."

There was a touch of pleading in her voice. "I hope you're not going to leave again."

"I'd like to stay, mama, but you'd better hear me out first. You might not want me here after you hear my story."

"There's nothing you can say that --"

"Wait. Let me finish." I told her I'd been stripping and then I paused.

"I don't care about that, Kya. We all do what we have to in order to survive."

"I'm pregnant, mama."

Her eyes lit up for an instant, then darkened. "Oh, baby, where's the father?"

"He's a wolf, like daddy. I'm going to bring another half-breed into the world."

"Don't say that."

"What's the difference? A rose by any other name…"

"I hate that word. You're a proud demiwolf, and you're not going anywhere. You'll stay with me and I'll help you raise the baby. Everything will be fine."

It was more than I could have hoped for.

* * *

Levi

I'm no coward. I'm an Alpha for fuck's sake, but the way I danced around Delilah sure made me feel gutless. Instead of asserting myself and demanding that she go along with my wishes, I lied and told her I'd be a faithful mate. The whole situation didn't sit right with me. I wanted to put her in her place or send her packing. Only respect for the elders kept me from doing it.

I was already in a pissed-off mood when I left home for Show 'n Tails, determined to make Raven a kept woman. There'd be no commitment, just fucking. Raven knew the score. She could never be my wife, meet my family, or bear my children. In return, I'd make things easy for her, a nice apartment, food, clothes. She wouldn't have to work. All she'd have to do is be there when I wanted her.

I'd find her a place closer to my home because getting out of the house was going to be a bitch. Delilah was already making things tough for me. Today I'd told her she'd be on her own because I was going to the city to look for a wedding tux. Of course, she wanted to come. "Absolutely not," I told her. "I want to pick out my own suit." Then I left before she could protest. For the first ten miles, I kept looking over my shoulder, because I thought she'd follow me. When I knew I was on my own, I felt like a ball and chain had been removed from my ankle.

By the time I got to the club, it was early evening. The manager remembered me; we must have spread a lot of money around. He started to lead me to a table, but I stopped him.

"Is Raven working?"

"No, but you'll love Scarlet, a gorgeous redhead with --"

Shit. "When will Raven be on?"

He kept trying to change the subject, but I refused to be distracted. "I want to see Raven."

"No can do. The bitch quit. One day she didn't show up and I never saw her again."

Bitch? I wanted to punch his lights out but I needed more information. "I need her address, and her real name."

His beady eyes regarded me closely. "I can't do that."

I held up a twenty. "Sure you can."

"How do I know you won't hurt her?"

I added a fifty. "Trust me. I just want to talk to her."

He grabbed the money and shoved it in his pocket. "I have to look it up."

I followed him into the office and tapped my foot impatiently while he checked the computer. Finally, he wrote something on a piece of paper and handed it to me. Kya Brewer. *Kya.* It suited her. I liked it better than Raven. Without a word, I turned my back on the sleazeball and stomped out.

I just hoped she was okay. *If someone hurt her…* I set my GPS to Kya's address and it led me to a tenement building in a crime-ridden neighborhood rife with abandoned housing, poverty, and drugs, the streets littered with garbage. Groups of idle teenagers hung on the corners. The building's façade was flat against the street and covered with rows of fire escapes, exterior iron balconies connected by iron ladders. What a dump. I kept imagining how grateful she'd be when I moved her out.

The lock on the front door didn't work. I walked inside with no problem. A long, dirty hallway ran straight from front to back and apartment doors lined both sides. No elevator. I headed up the stairway, careful of the broken banisters, and found apartment 401.

I knocked. No answer. I started pounding on the door. Frustrated, I tried the doorknob, surprised when it opened easily. It worried me that someone might have broken in and hurt Kya.

"Kya, are you home?"

I didn't have to look far to see that she wasn't. It was a tiny flat with a daybed, a hotplate, and a mini fridge. I checked the bathroom. Everything had been cleaned out. Her clothes, makeup, everything. She hadn't just left work, she'd left town. My guilt increased. Had she left because of me? It didn't matter. I had to find her.

Tracking came naturally to me. I started as a young pup and refined my natural instincts as I got older. Normally, I shifted to wolf form and worked with my nose to the ground. This time would be different. I assumed Kya had driven, or taken a bus, so I'd be air-scenting from my car.

Kya's scent was already implanted in my brain, but I sniffed her bedding to reinforce it. Once learned, I can follow a scent regardless of the other smells I encounter on a trail. If I had to get a job, I could be one hell of a detective. My nose can pursue prey 130 miles, or more.

Anxious to get started, I left the building and got in my car. I picked up Kya's scent on the air currents. Now to find its origin.

Kya's scent led me to Philadelphia. I'd never been there before, but those inner city neighborhoods all looked the same. My sensitive nose objected to the garbage spilling out into the street and the rank bodies of the homeless blocking my path. Everything I witnessed made me yearn for the unspoiled landscape of Adirondack Park. I just knew Kya would love it. An image of us running together crossed my mind, and I realized I didn't even know if she could shift.

I sighed and stopped to get my bearings. *Yes, this is the street.* I parked my Range Rover and got out. A young tough jostled me as I passed him. I ignored him and kept walking. The next thing I knew, I had a gun at my back. This cocky bastard was attacking me in broad daylight and on a public street.

I was enraged. The fight or flight reflex doesn't apply to me. An Alpha never runs. I rely on instinct and I use my head as well as my muscles. First, I had to disarm the creep. I raised my hands. "Look, I don't want any trouble."

"Good. Just hand over your keys."

He poked me hard with his weapon, and I knew instantly it was no gun. Luck was on my side. "They're in my pocket."

"Take them out slow and easy."

I slipped my hand in my pocket and maneuvered

the key until it was between my fingers. In an instant, I whirled around and slashed the mugger's cheek with the key. He screamed, dropped his weapon, and covered his face. I looked down. A screwdriver lay at my feet. Really?

The asshole wouldn't give up. He came at me, fists flying. I blocked his blows, easily fending off anything he could throw, and anticipating the right moment to counter. The opening came and I took it, delivering a punch that caught him square in the jaw. He staggered backwards and went down from the force of the blow. Stunned, he sat there holding his bloody face and staring up at me. I hauled him up by his shirt and slammed him against a brick wall. He winced at the impact.

"Next time think twice before you screw with somebody." I released him and he slid down the wall. I pictured him with his jaw wired shut. It was a satisfying image. Then I turned away to follow Kya's scent.

Chapter Four

Kya

The doorbell rang relentlessly. Mama must have forgotten her keys again. I stepped out of the shower and wrapped a towel around myself. "I'm coming."

I padded barefoot to the door and looked through the peephole. A girl couldn't be too careful in this neighborhood. *Levi?* My body stiffened in shock. One look at his handsome face awoke all the emotions I'd tried to bury. We'd had so little time together, but how could I forget him when I carried his scent and his child close to my heart? I wanted to talk to him, but fear kept me still. How had he found me? And more importantly, why? Did he somehow know I was pregnant?

The bell rang again and again. "I know you're in there, Kya. I can smell you. I'm not leaving until you open the door."

Oh, God. I didn't want him here when my mother got home. Better to get this over with now. "Just a minute. I'm not dressed." I realized how stupid that sounded after what we'd done, but I didn't want to face him wearing just a towel. Quickly, I threw on my sweats and opened the door.

Levi reached out for me, but I backed away. "How did you find me?"

He grinned and touched his nose. "I can always find you, Kya." He took a step closer. "You can find me, too. Whenever you need me."

I felt tears coming on. Damn hormones. I set my face in a hard mask. "I'm fine. I don't need you."

"You're not fine. Not in this place. Some thug tried to mug me when I got out of my car."

"Are you all right?" I gasped, couldn't help

myself.

"I can take care of myself. It's you I worry about. Can I sit down?"

I nodded reluctantly and waved at one of my mother's threadbare chairs. I sat opposite him. An awkward silence followed while I twisted my damp, tangled curls around my fingers. I'd imagined meeting Levi again, but now that it was actually happening, I had no idea how to react. And he'd caught me at my worst.

In contrast, he looked amazing, so incredibly hot that he took my breath away. I'd never even seen him naked, but I just knew his body would be perfect. His facial scruff, dark eyes, and long lashes were so sexy, I lost myself in his masculine beauty. I almost wished for a son, a beautiful boy who would look just like Levi, but a constant reminder of the man who stole my virginity and my heart would be torture. Damn Raven and my hormones. How could I want to destroy this man and fuck him at the same time?

"Why did you run away, Kya?"

I looked up in surprise. "My life is none of your business, Levi. Why are you here?"

For an instant, wistfulness stole into his expression. "I miss you. I think about you all the time."

His answer stunned me. For a second I allowed myself to believe it was true. A twinge of nausea reminded me of the secret I carried. Maybe we could be a real family. I opened my mouth to tell him about the baby, and then I remembered how we met. "Did you break your engagement?"

"Not exactly." A sheepish look came over his face.

Warily, and wearily, I waited for the other shoe to drop.

"I'm getting married in a few days, but I want to settle things between us first."

I wasn't surprised, but I swear an arrow pierced my heart. I reminded myself that he didn't belong to me. He never had.

"I'm not good with words, but I do care about you, Kya."

Damn him. I was finally building myself back up. Why did he have to show up now?

"I want to help you."

"How? By giving me more money to appease your conscience?"

"It's not like that. I want you in my life."

"But you're marrying another woman."

"It's complicated. I don't have a choice."

"There's always a choice."

He shook his head. "Listen, I've worked this all out so it's best for everyone. I can fulfill my duty to the pack and still take care of you."

I was confused, and I couldn't think straight. Looking at Levi opened up the hole he'd left in my heart.

"I want to move you out of this dump. I'll find you a place near me, somewhere in the mountains where it's safe, and I'll pay for everything."

Oh my God. He wanted to make me his whore. I was speechless.

He must have taken my silence for acceptance because he continued talking. "I'll see you whenever I can, and there are just a few ground rules for you to follow. You will not be involved with my family or the pack. No discussing my personal life or my wife, ever."

"Let me get this straight," I said tonelessly. "Our relationship will be strictly sexual. No strings for you, but I will be at your beck and call. I expect you'll have to make plans at the last minute or cancel them at a moment's notice, depending on your personal life."

He smiled. "I'm glad you understand."

"Get out."

Levi looked confused. "What?" He stood and tried to reach for me.

I snarled and drew back my lips. "Get the fuck out. If you come back, I'll kill you."

Levi growled. "You ungrateful bitch." He straightened his shoulders and turned away, pausing at the door. "You're passing up a good opportunity. This could be a new start for you, Kya. I'll give you some time to think it over, and I'll get back to you."

"There's nothing to think about." I slammed the door in his face.

In some ways my life would be easier if I went along with Levi's plan, but I never considered it for a second. Not even for the sake of my baby. My own father had died defending me. That was the kind of father I wanted for my son or daughter, not a man who would keep us hidden from his family and friends. What kind of role model would I be if I became a kept woman?

My life had never been easy, but I'd always gotten by. Somehow, I'd make it all work. This time I'd have my mother with me. Between us, we'd give this baby all the love it deserves. And someday, when my child asks about his father, I'll tell him he's a handsome, powerful Alpha. I'll just leave out the fact that he's an arrogant, egotistical, jerk. My eyes got misty.

Stop acting like such a complete and utter crybaby.

I buried my emotions and thought about my next move. Raven was my backbone. She'd gotten into my head and helped me stand up to an Alpha, but now we were all in danger, and I needed a plan. We'd have to run, but where? If Levi wanted to find me, he would.

I heard Mama opening the door. I didn't want to lie, but I needed a good reason to run. Borrowing Levi's story, I started crying and collapsed in her arms. "Mama, something bad happened. I was mugged in the street. It's not safe here. We need to move."

She didn't believe my lie about being attacked, not for a minute. "Tell me what really happened, baby."

Finally, I admitted that the father of my child had tracked me down. "He'll be back, I'm sure of it, and I'm afraid of what he might do. We need to leave. As soon as possible."

Mama seemed sad. She couldn't look me in the eye. "You're right, baby. I know a place where you'll be safe, but I can't go with you."

"What?" My heart started racing. "I won't go without you."

"You have to. It's the only way." She put up a hand to stop my protests. "Listen to me. When you left home, I went to a friend of your father's. He was a shifter, but sympathetic, and he told me about a place where demiwolves created a safe haven for themselves. They don't accept wolves or humans."

She smiled at the surprised look on my face.

"Yes, there are many more like you. I don't know how many. They wouldn't let me in. I drove for eight hours, and they refused to talk to me. They would only say that if you were there you were well protected. I used to pretend that you were living there and happy. It was easier than imagining you in trouble or worse."

"But I'm afraid for you, too, mama."

"Think of the baby. I have some money put away, enough for a plane ticket. If you fly there, the wolf will not be able to track you."

"But if he comes back --"

"If he comes back, I'll set him on a wild goose chase. What can your Alpha do to an old woman?"

I didn't want to go anywhere without her, but she refused to make a move. In the end, I agreed that her idea was the best. I needed to think of my child and take charge of our future. "You're right, Mama. I promise we'll come back for you."

* * *

Levi

Devastated, I sat in the car and tried to figure out what had gone wrong. I'd thought we had a connection. I thought Kya would accept my proposal, but anything I said just pushed her further away. There was no understanding women. We operated on logic. They operated on emotion.

My only option was to give Kya some space and let her think it over. If she were smart, she would come to her senses and accept my arrangement. In the meantime, I'd go home and marry Delilah. It wasn't what I wanted, but I had to follow the program.

If my future hadn't been mapped out for me, I could have what I wanted -- a happy life with a mate who respected and adored me. Clearly, that wasn't Delilah. Too bad she wasn't more like Kya.

Seeing Kya again made me realize just how much I missed her. Despite the fact she'd rejected me and thrown me out of her apartment, her strong will impressed me. She possessed all the traits of a wolf -- strength, initiative, a desire for freedom, beauty, pride... Life was so unfair. If Kya weren't a demiwolf she'd have the world at her feet.

It made me wonder what Kya wanted out of life.

The thought nagged at me. What if Kya wanted the same things I did? Suddenly it all made sense. I'd hurt her pride. Instead of showing her affection and respect, I'd treated her like a piece of property. But, what else could I have done? In a perfect world, I'd marry Kya, fuck her 24/7, and have lots of babies. In our society, it could never happen.

The closer I got to home, the more I dreaded it. The thought of living with Delilah became unbearable. I'd rather spend my life alone than with a woman who was negative and overbearing. Delilah was sucking the life out of me. I needed to confront the situation head on and break our engagement. My father wouldn't be happy, but I'd just have to make him understand that we weren't compatible.

I started writing a speech in my head.

"I do care for you, Delilah, but... you're an emotional vampire and I'm tired of being drained."

Ha! That's what I wanted to say. In reality, I would take the blame, and let her down easy.

"In the short time we've spent together I've come to realize we're not compatible. It's my failure, not yours. You're too good for me and you don't deserve a life with someone who won't make you happy."

I committed the speech to memory and drove directly to my parents' home, where Delilah was staying. When I got there, I saw her sitting on the front porch reading. I joined her, and she offered to get me a drink.

"No, thank you. I need to tell you something."

Delilah nodded politely. "Actually, I've wanted to talk to you, too. But you go ahead."

God, we sounded so formal, not at all like an engaged couple, which we soon wouldn't be. "Ladies first." I wasn't being gallant, just putting off the inevitable for a few more minutes.

"I spoke to my mother earlier. They've booked their flights. My parents will be here in a few days and you don't seem to care about the wedding planning at all. Is that a reflection of how much you care about our relationship?"

I took a deep breath, opened my mouth, and couldn't remember a damn word of my speech.

"Well? Say something."

Shit. I'll just ad-lib. "It's a bad relationship."

Delilah's eyes bugged out of her head. "Really? And whose fault is that?"

I shrugged. "You can blame me if you want, but the truth is we don't really know each other and we're not compatible. I should have seen it sooner, but I was trying to please everyone except myself. No more. I can't keep letting other people dictate what I do with my life."

"That's just like you to think of yourself. You're selfish and… and mean."

"And I'm not ready to tie the knot. I'm breaking up with you."

"You can't do that."

"I just did."

"Fuck you! I should probably thank you. You don't want a partner, you want a housekeeper and a baby machine. You're domineering and aggressive, and you'd be a lousy husband."

"Delilah, you're right. I am who I am. I can't apologize because I was born to lead the pack."

Still sputtering, Delilah started to walk away. Then she turned back. "Just so you know, I'm keeping the ring. You owe me big time for all the years I wasted waiting for you."

"I don't want it back." God, I felt so relieved.

"Keep the clothes, gifts, everything --"

Delilah disappeared into the house, the door slamming behind her.

Chapter Five

Kya

Eight months ago, I found Utopia. That's what they call the commune in West Virginia. It wasn't easy to find. The place was well hidden, but I followed my mother's directions and eventually reached a gatehouse at the entrance. At first, the guard turned me away. I begged for asylum and eventually he called the Stewards to join us. The Stewards are a group of six who, with community feedback, manage the property and affairs of Utopia. They took me in, but there were conditions. I had to take a DNA test and they kept me in quarantine until the results came back. Only when they were sure of my parentage did I become a full member of the community.

Utopia is nestled deep in the woods. It houses some eighty demiwolves, young and old, male and female. Life is good, but not perfect. Utopia is meant to be a quiet refuge, without the stress of society, but we're surrounded by a very high electrified fence. I feel like a prisoner. Essentially I am.

I quickly lost touch with the outside world. We have Internet, but it's only used for business. Some of the people here are artisans and they sell their furniture, crafts, and clothes online. Some are nurses, others are teachers, and everyone utilizes their skills.

Mostly, we live off the land, eating what we grow ourselves. It turned out that I have a green thumb, so I help tend the gardens. We share everything, including housing. I live in a large cabin with ten others. My bedroom is mine, but we share the bathrooms, kitchen, and common areas.

It's a very different world than I'm used to. We're all the same, misfits who wanted a place where we'd be accepted. I learned a lot living with my own kind. Now I know I'm not crazy. I've accepted Raven as a part of myself -- maybe the best part. She's the animal spirit in my mind and body, and we're learning to work in unity.

These demiwolves have taught me to love and respect myself. There's a real sense of support and community here, but I miss my solitude. I've always been a loner. I guess it goes back to growing up with parents who demanded privacy, and not having any friends. If I stay here, my child will never lack for friends, but living in Utopia doesn't come without sacrifice. My child and I will never see my mother again, or the outside world. An image of Levi torments me, but I block it. I'm safe, but I'm a prisoner inside a limited reality. It's a trade-off I'm not sure I'm willing to make.

But for now, sitting on my bed and counting the minutes between contractions, I'm where I need to be.

A knock sounded on the door, and Nurse Marta poked her head in. "Just checking. How are you doing?"

I gasped and hit the stopwatch. The pain began in my lower back and moved toward my belly. It lasted a minute. "Okay." Three minutes later, it started again. Panting, I got up and held onto the footboard. Suddenly, a flood gushed from between my legs.

"It won't be long now," Marta said, cheerfully. She spread pads over the bed and told me to lie down.

I thought of Levi, again. He should be here. I wanted him here. Then my labor began in earnest and I forgot everything else. Thank God for Marta. She told me when to push and I followed her directions.

"Ease up now, Kya," she said. "Your baby is crowning."

The rest followed so quickly. Soon Marta was exclaiming, "You have a boy." She put him in my arms and I fell in love.

He looked so like his father it made my heart ache. Those dark eyes, framed by long black lashes, locked on mine. Seconds later, he started rooting at my breast for milk. I clutched him to my chest, and swore I would do anything to protect him.

"What will you call him?" Marta asked.

"Levi. I'll call him Levi."

* * *

Levi

I gave Kya a week to calm down and then I went back to talk. I couldn't ask her to marry me, but at least I could tell her I was a single man. It never occurred to me that Kya would do another runner.

When I returned to Philly an older woman answered my knock. It shocked the hell out of me.

"I'm here to see Kya."

"Kya doesn't live here."

Tamping down my impatience, I kept my voice steady. "What are you talking about? I just saw her last week."

The woman crossed her arms over her chest. "I'm Claire, her mother. She was visiting and now she's gone."

I could see the resemblance. Something tightened in my chest. "Where? I need to talk to her."

"Canada. We've been told they're more tolerant there."

"Do you have an address? A phone number?"

"No, but that's Kya's way. She's independent."

I halfway believed her. I knew Kya had spirit. "If you hear from her will you give her a message? Tell her I care for her and I only want the best for her."

Kya's mother nodded, but she looked skeptical.

"I'll keep in touch." Then I thanked her and l left.

Kya's trail led me to the airport. She could have gone to Canada. Then again, she could have gone anywhere. No one would give me any information, and believe me, I asked. I was almost arrested for causing a disturbance.

Since then, I've visited Kya's mother twice, hoping to catch Kya there. Her mother always tells me she hasn't heard from her. I'm not sure I believe her, but I won't give up.

My father was pissed. He tried to make another match for me, but word got around. I've been deemed unsuitable. It's just as well.

I've had a lot of time to think and now I know what I want -- Kya. Nothing else matters, not even being Alpha. God, what an idiot I was. Why didn't I listen to my heart? My wolf spirit mated Kya, but I thought I could have my cake and eat it too.

Now I know Kya is my mate. She's the woman that I should have ended up with but didn't because I was a real dick-swinging Neanderthal. Damn, I'm totally in love and it sucks, because Kya doesn't feel the same. If only I could go back in time, I'd give her all the love and respect she deserves. Kya is the one that got away, but I'm determined to get her back.

I started throwing clothes into my duffle bag. It was time to visit Kya's mother again. Maybe this time I'd get lucky. I'm not hopeful. The universe works in mysterious ways. I'd wanted a wife and a mistress. In the end, I got neither. Karma? Maybe. Maybe justice was being served. What goes around comes around. I might be alone for the rest of my life.

* * *

Kya

Levi Junior is the perfect baby. He rarely cries, and he nurses every four hours. Surrounded by so many doting *aunts and uncles*, he basks in their delighted approval. My baby is happy, but I'm not. Whenever someone holds him, I'm consumed by guilt because his grandmother doesn't even know he's been born.

The Stewards would not permit my mother to visit. They said it would open the floodgates to disaster. Everyone would demand visiting privileges for friends and relatives and we'd all be put at risk. I knew I had no choice. I had to visit my mother. Everyone tried to dissuade me, but my mind was made up. I borrowed money for the plane fare and assured them I'd be back.

* * *

What a trooper. Junior slept as if the plane was his own personal flying cradle. My flight was not so peaceful. I'd called my mother from the airport to tell her I was coming. She was happy, but I heard the nerves in her voice.

She told me that Levi had returned for me. Several times, in fact. He even left messages saying he cared for me. I believed he cares, just not enough. Our physical connection was real, primal and fierce in a way that transcended anything I could have imagined, but he didn't respect me. He made me feel low, as if I meant less than nothing. I would never be good enough for him or his pack. So why did he come back? The answer was simple, Levi was a man who always got what he wanted and he could not take no for an answer.

But he hadn't been back recently. Mama thought

he might have given up. I thought so, too. After all, he must be starting his own family by now. The thought made my heart ache. *We're his family.* No, I told myself. We would just be his dirty little secret. It still hurt. I'd been away for the better part of a year, but I hadn't lost my desire for my baby's father. Could I resist if he came for me? I was stronger now.

It was a short flight. The attendant told us to fasten our seatbelts and put our seats in the upright position. We were getting ready to land.

Junior yawned and stretched. "I hope you don't miss Utopia too much," I whispered. He looked toward the window, and then he smiled at me as if to say, "I'm happy wherever you are." There was love and purity in his gaze. I kissed his dear sweet cheek. "I love you, Levi."

The plane touched down and my heart lurched. Was I making a mistake? It's just a visit, I told myself.

A short ride in the taxi and I was banging on Mama's door. She opened it and swept us into her arms. She laughed, she cried, all her worry lines disappeared. "He's so beautiful, Kya. I just want to hold him forever."

Junior seemed enchanted with her. I knew I'd done the right thing.

Mama cuddled him while I told her stories of Utopia. Her eyes went wide. "It really does sound like a utopia. Maybe you've found your true home, Kya."

"I don't know." A sadness crept over me. "I feel like a part of me is missing."

"Oh, baby. I know what that feels like."

Junior started wailing and I reached for him. "That's a hungry cry. I need to change him, too."

"Let's take him in the bedroom. There's diapers and a place for him to sleep."

My jaw dropped. Next to the bed was a wooden rocking cradle. "Where did you get this?"

"It's yours, baby. Your father made it. I couldn't bear to part with it. It's been in the basement storage room all these years. I cleaned it up for my grandson."

My eyes clouded. "It's perfect."

Mama wiped her own eyes. "Feed him, Kya, while I fix something for us."

She closed the door behind her and I settled on the bed with Junior. He latched on to my breast immediately and his tiny fingers grasped mine. He was so trusting. I never knew I could love anyone so much.

* * *

Levi

How long could I keep doing this? Sooner or later I'd have to accept the fact that Kya might be gone forever. The thought made me sick. There was so much more that needed to be said. I needed closure.

When Kya disappeared, she pulled the rug out from under me. Crazy as it sounds, I felt abandoned. My life went to hell. I actually took Delilah's advice and delegated more duties to my beta. Even my father got involved.

The old man and I started talking more. He admitted he might have made a mistake choosing Delilah for me. When he met my mother, he let lupine instinct take over, and they had a match made in heaven. "Your wolf spirit knows better than me," he said. "But if you give in to your inherent biological needs and wants, you'll have to challenge the pack consensus. Are you prepared to do that?"

"Yes." I'd grown up. Despite our differences, I knew Kya and I were perfect for one another.

* * *

Kya

I jumped when I heard a loud knocking at the apartment door. Levi Junior picked up on my agitation immediately and he started crying.

My mother appeared at the bedroom door, her face pinched and ashen. "It's him. Should I call the police?"

"It won't help. He hasn't done anything."

"Yet," she added, with a little cry.

The knocking turned into banging. "Let me in. I know you're there."

My pulse quickened, but I was determined to stay calm for my mother and the baby. What doesn't break you makes you stronger. I could handle this. The man on the other side of the door might not love me, but he wasn't a threat. "Let him in, Mama. He won't hurt us."

My mother paused uncertainly, then left the bedroom and shut the door behind her. Junior cried louder. I cuddled him to my breast and tried to calm him.

* * *

Levi

I smelled Kya inside the apartment, and something else. A baby cried, confirming my suspicions. Blood roared in my ears. I wouldn't let her get away again. Determined, I got ready to kick the door down. It opened suddenly and Kya's mother stood there, trembling with fear.

"I want to see her."

"Please don't hurt them."

Her words made me angry. "I would never. I love her."

Claire stepped aside and I swept past her, and through the empty living room. I opened the bedroom door and all the blood inside me rushed to my heart. *I'm a father.* There was never any question that the baby was mine.

Kya met my gaze and for a long moment we stared at each other. I tried to read her expression but it was complicated. I saw anger, but something else as well. It gave me hope.

"I told you not to come back, Levi."

"I had no choice."

Kya sighed. "There's always a choice."

She was right, of course. "Yes. I could ache for you the rest of my life, or keep looking for you. I chose to keep looking." I couldn't take my eyes off the baby suckling at her breast. "Were you ever going to tell me? I have a right to see my child."

"How do you know he's yours?"

I couldn't help grinning. "I have a son?"

Kya nodded. "Do you acknowledge him?"

"Yes." Raw with embarrassment, I took a step closer. "I want to see him."

Kya nodded toward the side of the bed and I sat down. Being this close to her was sheer torture. I wanted to touch her so bad.

The baby released her breast and looked at me. A rush of warm emotion flooded my body. "Can I hold him?"

Kya hesitated before handing the baby to me.

"I'll be careful." He settled into my arms, pursed his lips and gave me a big sloppy smile.

Kya smiled, too. "He's milk drunk. He'll be asleep soon."

"Kya, look what we made." I felt the bond grow between this cub and me, and it was a force of nature. I hooked for life. I started singing to him. "Sleep, little lobo, don't you howl, daddy's going hunting…" I hummed a bit more and looked up. Kya was staring at me. I shrugged. "I forgot the rest. It's been a long time since I heard it. Twenty-five years."

* * *

Kya

Never did I picture Levi singing lullabies to our son. This made things much more difficult for me. It broke my heart.

"What did you name him, Kya?"

"Levi, Junior."

Levi's eyes went wide with shock.

I shrugged. "I suppose you'll have another Junior, but it doesn't matter. They'll never meet."

Levi put Junior in the cradle and tucked him in. Then he reached for me. I pulled away. "No."

Levi sighed. Pain etched lines in his face. "I never meant to hurt you."

"Well, you did." I refused to let him stomp on my heart again. "But I'm okay. We live with others like us, in a beautiful place called Utopia. I just brought the baby back for a visit, so there's no need to worry about us running into your real family."

"You are my real family. There is no other Junior and there never will be. There's no other woman. Only you, Kya. You're my mate. I love you."

Did I hear right? My head went swimmy. "I don't know what to say."

"Say you love me, too. Say you want to be with me. Say you want to raise our son together. Say --"

"Stop." I couldn't bear it. "You're lying. We're too different. You know we can't be together."

"I'm not lying. I wanted you the first time I laid

eyes on you. I thought it was all about sex, but my wolf knew better. I should have listened. You're my other half, Kya. When I'm with you, I feel like anything is possible. I never felt that way about another woman. I had nothing in common with the she-wolf my father picked for me."

"What do we have in common, Levi?"

He looked over at Junior.

"There has to be more."

"There is. We both want the same things, Kya, a home filled with love, respect, trust, someone to laugh with, someone to cry with. I want it all, with you."

It sounded wonderful. If only we could live in the moment and not think about the future, but I had a child now. I always loved my father and I had accepted his origins. I loved Levi, and I could embrace his parentage, but could he do the same for Junior and me? Could he live with the bigotry of his pack, or would he grow to resent us?

"Your pack would never accept me, or my son. They'll call him a half-breed."

Levi winced. "Our son, Kya. He's mine, too." He tilted my chin up, so I was looking into his eyes. "Look at me, Kya. I can't live without you. I don't give a fuck about the pack."

"Don't lie to me."

He hesitated. "I'm not. Of course, I worry about the pack, but you and our baby come first. My parents have already told me they'll welcome you into our family as their daughter-in-law. I'm over the moon about the baby. I have no doubt they will be, too. If anyone disrespects you or Junior, they'll answer to me."

My heavy heart lightened a little. Maybe there was hope for the future. "I want our child to grow up accepting his human side as well as his wolf."

"I promise you that he will. I've learned a hard lesson. I know we're just as guilty of bigotry and hatred as the humans. We all have good and bad inside us and the only way we'll ever live in peace and be happy is if we put our differences aside and accept each other. My son will grow up believing that."

My doubt dissolved and I got all misty. Levi brushed a tear from my face. I grabbed his hand and held his palm to my cheek. Kissed it.

"I'd give my life for you and Junior. Can you forgive me for being an arrogant prick, and --"

I pressed my lips to his.

"Kya," he breathed.

My heart fluttered at the sound of his voice. He traced my lips with his tongue and I opened for him. Our kiss was hot and fiery, demanding as hell. It knocked the breath out of my lungs. I threw my arms around his neck, gasping at the heat of our contact.

Levi drew back and studied my face. I stared back. The emotion I saw in his expression shocked me. It told me more than words that he really loved me.

I unbuttoned his shirt and ran my fingers over his chest, coaxing a shiver out of him. "Strip for me," I murmured.

"No way."

"I want to see your body." I pouted. "I did it for you."

"I paid you," he protested.

I smiled mischievously. "You'll be well paid."

"I'm not a dancer." Levi frowned, but he stood. "Remember, you asked for this." He took off his shirt.

The dark curls between his pecs, and his sculpted abs made my mouth water, but I wanted more. "Act sexy."

He threw me a dirty look before turning his back. Then he shoved his jeans over his slim hips and kicked them aside. Bending over like I'd done on the stage, he wiggled his ass. I clapped and whistled, then I clamped a hand over my mouth. I'd almost forgotten about Junior.

Levi turned to face me and he winked. "Better?"

"Much."

He strutted around the bedroom, his cock swelling and growing stiff. Evidently, showing his stuff was a turn-on. It was for me, too. His walk slowed. He stood at the foot of the bed while I admired his hairy, muscular legs, and perfect cock, surrounded by a wild bush. He started stroking himself and I bit my lip. It was so incredibly fucking hot.

I beckoned him with a crooked finger. "Come here."

Levi flashed me a wicked smile and jumped on the bed beside me. "How did I do?"

"You're a natural." I kissed him on the lips.

"I'll do anything to make you happy, Kya."

"Do I make you happy?"

He groaned and pulled me to him. "The only time I'm happy is when I'm with you."

I wanted him more than ever. The need to have him inside me overpowered everything. "I want you."

"Oh, God. I want you, too. So much." He growled and reached for my breast. "They've grown a bit," he muttered hoarsely.

"Stop complaining. They're feeding your child."

Levi chuckled. "I'm not complaining. In fact, I may just keep you barefoot and pregnant all the time."

"It'll never happen. You talk too much."

"Hah! I have a feeling you won't let me get a word in."

He kissed me then, and left a trail of fire from my mouth to my breast. Groaning, I gripped his hair when he swirled his tongue around a nipple, then sucked gently.

"God, you're beautiful. So sexy and curvy. I wish I could have been with you when you were pregnant."

"Be careful what you wish for. Morning sickness and backaches are not very sexy. But I loved all of it, except for missing you."

"You won't miss me next time. I'll be there so much you'll be sick of me."

"I could never be sick of you. And we have so much time to make up."

He slid a finger inside my pussy and moved it in and out like a cock. His touch was so gentle that I moaned deep in the back of my throat. I was on fire. "Stop teasing me."

"I promise to deliver."

Levi kneeled between my thighs and pushed them apart. I shuddered when I felt his mouth on me, his rough tongue teasing my clit before plunging inside me. My hunger rose hard and fast. I whimpered and begged him for release. Finally, he sucked my swollen clit into his mouth and I came like never before. Rising over me, Levi swallowed my moans with a kiss.

I wanted him to come, and I reached for his hard, swollen cock. It twitched as I rubbed precum over the head. I wrapped my fingers around the shaft and stroked the length until he started to pant, then I released him.

Levi loomed over me. His eyes were wild and hungry. His nostrils flared as fluid leaked from my pussy.

"I'm so empty without you. Fuck me, Levi."

"No." He growled at me. "I want to make love with you."

Those words touched my heart. "I want that, too."

Cupping my ass, he drew me closer and positioned himself at my weeping slit. "This time I want to see your face."

He pushed inside and the breath caught in my throat. Taking his time, he entered me slowly and gently, finally filling me completely. Then he pulled out and did it again.

I gasped with pleasure and urged him on. "Again, baby. You feel so good."

He started moving in a steady rhythm and I met each stroke. I tried to keep quiet but the room echoed with our animalistic growls and the scent of our sex inflamed me more.

He kept me on the edge until I begged for release. Then he pushed my clit and set off an earthshaking orgasm. I surrendered to it and as my body convulsed with waves of pleasure, he let out a possessive howl and pulled me against him. With a final thrust, he drove deep, coming hard and locking himself inside me. He sank his teeth in the soft flesh he'd bitten once before and rapture claimed me again.

Levi lowered himself on top of me and rolled us to our sides. His strong arms held me steady until I became coherent. I felt an intimacy I'd never experienced before, and I knew that our connection would bridge any cultural divide. "I love you," I told him, and then I laughed.

"What's so funny?"

"We're locked together, and I was just picturing Mama's face if we had to call her in here to get the baby."

Levi's expression turned horrified. "Oh, no."

"Don't worry, baby. My father was a wolf. She'll understand."

"I hope so." He pulled me closer. "You're mine now."

"I was always yours."

Levi cuddled me close, his arms encircling me. He drew me in for a kiss, his lips hungry for mine. In his embrace, my worries disappeared and my optimism grew, released by the love we shared. I smiled inside. I was lucky to have him, but he was lucky to have me, too. We were lucky to have each other.

Utopia had taught me so much. Instead of hiding in the commune, I'd convinced myself to venture out and be myself, unafraid and unapologetic. I'd held out for what I deserved and I'd gotten it. From now on, I would live proud, instead of ashamed.

"A penny for your thoughts?"

"I was just thinking about our future."

"Are you sure you won't miss Utopia?"

I shook my head. "This *is* my Utopia."

The Beta's Spitfire (Utopia 2)
Gale Stanley

Samson: Levi and I have always been best friends. Now he's the pack Alpha and I'm his beta, a.k.a. the man who cleans up after his shit storms. This one is a doozy. He dumped his intended bride, and now it's my job to take care of her while he goes off to find his soulmate. Delilah is beautiful, a real spitfire, and completely off limits. But she ignites a fire that makes my wolf sit up and howl.

Delilah: I was meant to be the mate of an Alpha, so l accepted an arranged marriage with Levi. But the arrogant jerk dumped me right before the wedding. I'm no damsel in distress, so I took off for New York to live a life of independence. Along the way, I was kidnapped and my situation became desperate. When Samson came to my rescue, I never expected him to claim me for himself.

Chapter One

Delilah

After Levi dumped me, my father called wanting to know our wedding date. When I told him there'd be no wedding, he went ballistic. "Arranged marriages between wolf-shifters don't fall apart at the last minute. What did you do to make Levi call it off?"

Of course daddy dearest would blame me. It was the story of my life. My father and I never got along. He blamed our arguments on the "F" word -- *feminism*. According to him, equality of the sexes ruined the mating game. "Any wolf-shifter worth his salt wants a submissive wife to take care of his needs. If he can keep her barefoot and pregnant, so much the better." If I'd heard it once, I'd heard it a hundred times. Maybe a thousand.

Levi was just like my father. I guessed that's why Daddy picked him for me. He thought once we were married, Levi would keep me in line. Well, the joke was on Daddy. Levi didn't even try to tame me. I asserted my independence and Levi balked. He gave me that tired old line, "It's not you, it's me."

Bullshit! I was sure there was more to it. I wasn't that naive. More than once, I smelled cheap perfume on him. I wasn't exactly blindsided, and I wasn't heartbroken, but I was miffed. After all, I'm a catch -- the daughter of an Alpha, I come from the Chicago Shifters, an old and very wealthy pack.

But, like I said, there was more than meets the eye here. My spunky spirit was just a convenient excuse for Levi to break our engagement. Yes, he hated the fact that I wanted to be an equal partner in our relationship. Levi would have preferred a doormat, but under normal circumstances, he would have gone along with the arrangement for the sake of tradition.

I was convinced Levi dumped me for another woman. I'd been in New York for weeks, living with his parents and getting to know the pack, but Levi had been gone most of the time. He might be the Alpha, but nobody has that much business out of town, especially when they're supposed to be getting ready for their wedding.

One thing I had learned was to trust my intuition. If I got a feeling that something was wrong, I didn't chalk it up to being paranoid. I meditated on it and looked for signs. Levi had all the signs. He was moody, uncommunicative, critical, and he never showed any interest in sex.

She-wolves are supposed to stay pure until the wedding, but rules are meant to be broken. My girlfriends back home all had arranged marriages, but they all fucked their grooms before they said "I do." I had expected I would, too, but Levi had no interest in fucking me. He had to be getting it somewhere else. No surprise there. Men cheat. But I expected him to at least show some interest in me. I wasn't exactly an ugly duckling. Even Levi's beta had eye-fucked me more than once. Samson thought I didn't notice, but I had seen him checking me out. I knew he was undressing me in his head and wishing he could really fuck me. It was hot as hell, but neither of us ever took it any further.

"Delilah. Are you still there? Answer me."

"Yes, Daddy." I took a deep breath. "It's probably for the best. Levi is arrogant and a cheater."

"He's a strong Alpha, an admirable man."

Oh, please. I couldn't help thinking of my mother. As a kid, I would run to her and complain about my father. She would say, "He's an Alpha, that's how they are. Respect him." Bullshit! Where was the respect for us? For all she-wolves? My mother knew he cheated, but she turned a blind eye. She was old school. I was the new generation.

I had no love for the human race, but I liked the way their women fought for equality. That's what I wanted for myself. I was sick of being considered a second-class citizen, when in reality, I was Alpha material. It was time for me to take charge of my life and make it happen.

"Well?" Father shouted, so loud it sounded as if he were there with me. "You've ruined everything. What do you have to say for yourself?"

As a child, I had to obey my father, but now I was a grown ass woman, and I refused to answer to him. "Not a damn thing."

My father started cursing. "Don't come home. I'll talk to Levi and his parents. We can fix this and --"

I slammed the phone down. No need to listen to him rant. I didn't intend to go back to Chicago anyway. I wouldn't tolerate his beastly behavior anymore. I liked it in New York, and Levi's parents were very sympathetic. They had told me I could stay with them as long as I wanted. I was sure they expect us to patch things up, but that wouldn't happen, even if Levi got down on his knees. Screw him. I wanted better for myself.

As far as I was concerned, there was no advantage to being married. The elders say marriage gives you status in the pack and having purebred pups perpetuates our race. I say it's a sexist fabrication to give men control. I didn't want to be tied down, a servant to my husband. What kind of happily ever after was that?

Not my kind. I wanted a career in Manhattan. I

could blend in with the humans and start a new life. Thank God I had insisted on college before marriage. My business degree would help me find a job. I just needed a little more time here so I could visit the city, go on interviews, and look for an apartment. When everything was set up, I'd make my move.

Just then, I heard Levi's mother calling me and I went downstairs to watch Rhona futz with dinner. She was old school too, cooking a big meal every night for her husband and Levi. She checked the roast beef and looked over at me. "Do you want to mash the potatoes?"

I smiled sweetly. "You do it so much better."

Rhona flashed a disapproving look in my direction and got to work. She whipped the potatoes, adding milk and butter until the consistency suited her. Then she handed me the bowl. "The way to a man's heart is through his stomach. Take these into the dining room, please."

Bullshit. What she really wanted to say was, "You're a lazy bitch. No wonder you can't keep a man." Rhona had tried to get me into the kitchen many times, but cooking was not my thing. Besides, Levi was more than capable of fending for himself, even if his mother had made him into a twenty-five-year-old baby. But I was relying on her hospitality, so I smiled and took the potatoes. "They look delicious."

I liked the dining room. It was cozy, yet elegant, and the wood furnishings echoed the world outside. The big oak table and matching chairs dominated the space. Levi's father had made them himself when they married.

I wasn't surprised to see that the table was set for three. Levi had left town a few days ago and hadn't returned.

Dinner was an awkward affair. After dessert, I said I was tired and wanted an early night. His parents exchanged glances as I left the table.

* * *

Samson

I've always been an early riser. Good thing too, because Levi left me a ton of work. I showered and dressed, then headed for Levi's house.

The front door opened to the living room, which had been converted to Levi's office. Despite the many shelves and file cabinets lining the white walls, the room remained in a perpetual state of clutter and disorganization. Sighing at the mess, I headed to his kitchen to make myself coffee. I took a few sips, and then carried my mug back to the office and placed it next to the desktop computer.

The computer was grimy and old, like everything else in Levi's office. I logged on and waited for it to power up. It took forever. I'd replaced the power supply, added RAM, and updated the operating system, but it was already obsolete. I had begged Levi to let me renovate the office, but we always had the argument. "The pack doesn't have money for nonessentials."

"Bullshit." I knew Levi wasn't tech savvy and he felt intimidated by computers. "Keeping up with technology *is* essential."

"My old man never used one when he was Alpha, and he did okay."

"Things are different today."

"Not for me, Samson. I'm a hands-on guy. I don't need a tricked up office and flashy equipment. When my father was Alpha he solved problems by using his head and real physical work, not these so-called laborsaving devices. All they do is keep an Alpha from interacting with his pack."

I gave up. "Okay, man. Whatever you say."

Even if Levi thought I was right, he would never admit it. Levi was my best friend, but he had a big ego and didn't take advice well, especially from his second in command. I was good enough for the grunt work and maintaining law and order, but when it came to running the pack, my opinions didn't count.

The rest of Levi's house wasn't much better than the office. To say it needed work was an understatement. The old clapboard two-story house sat next door to his parents' home and had been furnished with their castoffs, right down to the floral print couch. There were two bedrooms and a bath on the second floor.

I couldn't understand why he hadn't fixed the place up for his intended bride, but then Levi had never showed much interest in Delilah. The day she arrived he took off for some appointment and he'd been doing it ever since, leaving me to fill in as escort and bodyguard for the stunning redhead.

Delilah was a real looker. Smart as a whip, too. She-wolves are supposed to do as they're told, but Delilah had a mind of her own. Levi complained plenty about her independent streak. His Alpha ego demanded a more compliant mate. Not me. I wanted a strong woman I could talk to, an equal, a partner. But I wasn't likely to find one in our pack. We outnumbered the women two to one.

Tradition holds that a wolf will know his true mate, but with so few women to pick from, a guy can't rely on destiny. That's why Levi's father ignored the old ways and went outside the pack to find him a suitable mate. If I didn't choose a woman soon and start breeding, Levi might do the same for me.

Reproduction was a top priority for us. So was keeping the bloodline pure. I understood the reasons, but letting an Alpha pick my wife, even if he was my best friend, didn't appeal to me. Still, I was a loyal pack member and I'd probably go along with Levi's wishes like I always had.

Right now, that loyalty was a problem. Levi had me babysitting a woman I'd rather be fucking. Her scent drove me crazy, and every time I laid eyes on her, I got tongue-tied. He might not want her, but that didn't mean I could have her. According to the bro code a bro's ex-girlfriend is off-limits.

So here I was, drooling over Delilah, while I made up excuses to explain Levi's absence. I knew Delilah didn't believe me and I felt like a heel.

I was pretty sure he was fucking someone. We hold she-wolves to a strict standard of conduct. No sex until marriage. The same didn't hold true for our men. We could screw around as much as we wanted. It was hypocritical, but it was for the good of the pack, so no one disputed it. Except Delilah. I overheard her yelling at Levi once. She accused him of bringing her to the Adirondacks to be his broodmare. I had to bite my lip so they wouldn't hear me laughing. Like I said, she's feisty.

Sighing, I started putting together the end of the month financial reports. The keyboard had been used so much all the letters were worn off. Good thing I knew them by heart. One of the keys started sticking. Luckily, I was done.

I took a swallow of my coffee and listened to the voicemail. My ears perked up when I heard Levi's voice. Maybe he was coming home, finally.

"Hey, Samson, I'm on my way home and I'm

bringing my new wife. Uh, do me a favor, buddy. Can you straighten up the house? Thanks. I owe you one."

"What the fuck? You owe me a hell of a lot more than one, you son of a bitch."

To say I was stunned was an understatement. The only tail Levi had been chasing was the demiwolf he'd fucked at his bachelor party. She was one hot stripper, but he should have stuck with humans. Messing with a half-breed can get complicated. But it was his bachelor party, and, like I said, he never listened to me.

What should I tell his parents? And Delilah?

I smelled her before I saw her. Delilah's tantalizing scent hit me full force. My wolf stirred, randy and ready for business. I looked up and there she was, standing at the open door, the most beautiful creature I'd ever seen, a five foot four inch she-wolf with pale skin, flaming red hair, and bottle-green eyes. How could Levi have let her go?

Heat coiled in my belly, and I felt desire the likes of which I'd never felt before. I just sat there and stared as if I were in a hypnotic trance.

Delilah stormed toward the desk. "Don't just sit there drooling like a puppy."

"I… uh…" I shut my mouth, unable to get any words out.

"Have you nothing to say for yourself?"

"G-g-good m-m-morning, Delilah."

I felt my face heat, and I knew it was turning bright red. As a boy, I'd always had a hard time speaking when I was unsure of myself. The boys thought it was funny. They used to pound me on the back to help me get the words out. One day Levi stuck up for me, and no one bullied me again. We bonded that day, and became fast friends.

As I grew older, I overcame my stuttering, through hard work and focus, but the nerves and the stammering always seemed to come back when I was around Delilah.

* * *

Delilah

I was furious. "Don't 'good morning' me."

Samson's brown puppy-dog eyes opened wider. I could drown in those eyes, but I pulled my gaze away and strengthened my resolve. "Well?"

Finally, he stood up to greet me. Hands on hips, I confronted six feet four inches of lean muscle, with a mop of thick chestnut hair and chiseled features. His scent made me weak in the knees. I wanted to devour him like an apple cinnamon muffin. Too bad he was only a stuttering beta and not worth my attention.

"Would you like to s-s-sit down?"

"No, I would not. Let's not beat around the bush. I heard the message my philandering ex left for your ears only. Evidently, he plans on bringing his whore here to further embarrass me."

"I s-s-swear I didn't know anything about --"

I slammed my palm on the desk. "Bullshit. That arrogant jerk tells you everything. Who is she? Who is this she-wolf he's chosen over me?"

"S-s-she's not a s-s-she-wolf. She's a demiwolf."

"A *what*?" My pride was hurt and I felt flushed with the heat of my anger. "It's bad enough he dumped me for a half-breed, now he's bringing her here to humiliate me in front of everyone. How can I ever face my friends, my family, my father?"

"Let me get you s-s-some water, Delilah. We can work this --"

I walked out, slamming the door behind me. I

would never forgive Levi, and I sure as hell wouldn't stick around to meet his whore. It meant speeding up my departure, but it couldn't be helped.

I went next door and called out for Levi's parents. Nobody home. Perfect. I went upstairs to the guest room and packed in a hurry. I dragged my suitcase down the stairs and tried to formulate a plan. With everyone out, there was no car for me to borrow. I'd wheel my suitcase to the main road and call a cab, or catch a bus to the train station. Hopefully, no one would see me. I didn't want any questions because I wasn't going home.

My luck didn't hold out. Only one block away I ran into Milo. Like most gamma wolves he was a worthless horndog who contributed nothing to the pack, but he liked to party and fuck, so he and Levi got along fine. Milo was part of the Alpha's inner circle just like Samson, but there was no love lost between the gamma and the beta. They hid their mutual dislike from Levi, but I could see it clearly whenever they were together.

"Hey, little lady. Why are you dragging that heavy suitcase around?"

Shit. "Family emergency back in Chicago," I said over my shoulder while I kept walking. "I'll call a taxi from the main road."

Milo caught up with me easily and wrestled the suitcase from my grip. "Levi would never forgive me if I didn't give you a hand."

I spoke through gritted teeth. "It's really not necessary."

Milo ran a hand through his light brown hair and smiled at me as if I were a small helpless child. "Oh but it is. I'm not busy. I'd be happy to drive you to the train station." His grin didn't reach his eyes and I felt myself shrinking from his cold stare and shrewd smile.

I sucked it up. I didn't have much choice. "Well, if you really don't mind." I followed him and my suitcase over to his car and he helped me inside. While he stowed my luggage in the trunk, I tried to come up with a story.

Milo slid into the driver's seat. "Okay, little lady, we're off."

I wished I could smack the smarmy grin off his face and tell him how much I hated being called little lady, but I needed his good will. The only way to get that was to be flirty. I put my hand on his arm and fluttered my eyelashes. "Before we go, I need you to promise me one thing."

"Anything, little lady."

Inside I was cringing, but I wanted a head start, and I needed to buy some time. I knew Milo would have no problem keeping a secret from Samson. "I don't want anyone to worry about me, and if Samson knows I'm gone, he'll call Levi and raise an alarm. Please don't tell him you ran into me."

Milo leaned into me. I could feel his hot breath on my face. "I can sympathize. That dimwit is always hovering over you. I can't lie to him, but I can sure as hell avoid him for a while. If I don't see him, he can't ask me any questions. Will that help?"

"Yes. I really appreciate this."

"Now you owe me."

Try to collect, asshole. You'll never see me again. I gave a seductive smile, but inside I was seething.

Chapter Two

Delilah

I reached Penn Station with no problem, but the bustling train terminal was a sprawling mass of tracks, corridors, and concourses. The signs were bad and there were so many entrances to the street, I'd never been so confused in my life. I didn't want to ask for directions and risk calling attention to myself, so I chose an exit and found my way out.

I picked New York City because it has a large population and I could blend in easily, but my hasty departure meant I had a large suitcase with me and nowhere to stow it. I kept bumping into people on the crowded sidewalks and getting dirty looks in return. People eyed me as if I were a naïve tourist. I was neither. I knew I needed a place to stay ASAP and I started looking.

There were plenty of hotels, but one after another, I walked in, and walked out. They were way too expensive. I had money, but it wouldn't last long if I blew it all on a hotel. Spotting a place called Budget Hotel/Hostel, I crossed my fingers and went inside.

The pony-tailed guy at the desk was playing a computer game. He didn't even look up when I entered.

"Hello. I need a room."

"Hold on --"

I pushed the lid down on his laptop.

"What the fuck!" He finally raised his head. "You ruined my game."

"I need a private room."

This time he looked me over. A sly smile creased his lips. He gave me the creeps. "I just happen to have one available. It's on the third floor."

"How much?"

"Dirt cheap, but you have to share the bath."

"I'll take it." I paid in cash.

"I'm Bobby, by the way. The elevator is on the fritz. I'll help you with your bag."

"No need." But he was already up and grabbing my suitcase.

I followed Bobby up the fire stairs and down a dingy hall. He opened a door at the far end, and oh, my…

The room was tiny, like a coffin. I'm a wolf, used to open spaces. Nothing matched and the smell of smoke and sweat made me wrinkle my nose. I looked up. A dirty fan hung from the ceiling, but it looked so disgusting, I didn't plan on using it anytime soon. A huge cockroach disappeared under the bed. I wanted to leave, but I'd already paid and I needed a room. Tomorrow I'd look for a better place.

Bobby put my suitcase on the bed, which creaked loudly. I wondered if it would collapse under me. He shrugged his shoulders and grinned. His teeth were yellow. "It ain't much, but it's cheap and the subway is only a five-minute walk."

"It'll do."

When he realized he wasn't getting a tip, his smile disappeared. "The bathroom's down the hall." He slammed the door behind him.

I didn't unpack, just moved my suitcase to the floor so I could nap. I made sure the door was locked, then I pulled down the spread. The bed sheets were gray and they stunk. I called downstairs and asked Bobby for clean sheets.

"The laundry's not done yet. I'll leave a note for the housekeeper." He hung up.

Maybe I should have given him a tip. Too late

now. I just wanted to sleep, so I undressed and lay on top of the spread. Somehow, I fell asleep.

Agitated, my wolf moved inside me and I woke, groggy and disoriented. The room was dark and Bobby was looming over me, straddling me, his sour whiskey odor making me sick.

Animal instinct kicked in. Self-preservation is always my first thought. I do what I have to in order to survive. Pure adrenaline shot through me and I became the attacker, the beast, the wolf. My lips drew back, revealing a set of growing fangs, and I growled. Claws sprouted from my fingers as I swiped at his face.

Bobby's expression of horror would have been funny if I was inclined to laugh. Instead, I went for him again. His hands went to his bloody face and he backed off, nearly falling off the bed. "What the fuck are you?"

I realized my mistake and quickly took control of my wolf. "I'm a woman who protects herself. What makes you think you can walk into my room without knocking?"

"You bitch, I did knock. You didn't answer so I used my passkey to bring in your sheets."

"Bullshit. You came in the dark, uninvited, and when you saw me sleeping, you thought you could take advantage of me. You're pathetic."

Blood dripped through his fingers. "We'll see who's pathetic. You'll pay for this." He fled, and I immediately jumped up and shoved the lone chair under the doorknob. The lock wouldn't keep him out, but at least I'd hear him coming.

Now what? I didn't want to stay, but I didn't want to wander the streets at night, either. I'd wait until daylight, then shower and leave. I wouldn't sleep a wink the rest of the night.

* * *

Bobby

I checked out the damage in the mirror. That bitch had done a job on me. I needed stitches and I'd be scarred for life.

I'd heard of werewolves, but never believed they really existed, until now. Okay, I'd had a few drinks, but I know what I saw. And no ordinary woman had done this to my face. I wanted revenge, but I was scared shitless of confronting her. Maybe I wouldn't have to. *Tit for tat, lady.*

Working in this dump didn't cut it, so I supplemented my income by doing small jobs for the local drug syndicate. The mob boss also dabbled in sex trafficking. He'd pay big bucks for a looker like her. Kidnapping isn't my thing, but that redheaded bitch needed to be taught a lesson. I picked up the phone, told my contact what a beauty she was and warned him about the teeth and nails.

* * *

Delilah

I jerked awake. Somehow, I'd fallen asleep again and now morning light showed through the threadbare drapes. I should have just left but damn it, I'd paid for a shower. Throwing on sweats, I headed for the bathroom down the hall. All was quiet. Not a sound from any of the rooms I passed. I figured everyone was still asleep.

The bathroom was just as crummy as the rest of the place. The faded shower curtain hung from seven hooks instead of twelve. The towels were grayish looking and there was a bar of used soap. Fortunately, I had my own body wash and shampoo. This would be one quick shower.

I turned the water on high and waited for it to warm up. Finally, I undressed and stepped under the spray. Despite the circumstances, the hot water felt great. I rubbed shampoo into my hair and massaged my scalp. Closing my eyes, I let the water cascade through my hair.

I shouldn't have let my guard down. My wolf thrashed inside me, but it was already too late. Someone, a very big someone, tackled me from behind. I growled, but a muscular arm came round my neck and cut off any sound. My attacker pulled me out of the tub, dragging the shower curtain with me and trapping my arms in it. I used my claws to tear free and swipe at his face, but he slammed my head into the tiled wall. Overcome with pain, I slumped in his arms. A second man approached and I felt a prick in my neck.

After that, I saw everything in slow motion. I thought about my family. These men were going to kill me and I would never see my parents again. It pained me that the last time I had talked to my father we'd fought. I'd do anything for the chance to apologize.

"Bastards..." But my words trailed off. I felt dizzy and sluggish.

One of them put duct tape over my mouth. I shook my head, but it was no use. There wasn't an ounce of strength left in my body. They tied my wrists and ankles. One of the men lifted me. It was the last thing I remembered.

* * *

Samson

I had every intention of finding Delilah and trying to calm her down, but time just got away from me. Axel arrived shortly after Delilah stormed out. He had some crazy idea about starting a tech company to raise money. Well, being an omega wolf, and the brains of the pack, he's always pushing some new idea. I usually enjoyed hearing them, but today I had other things on my mind. Unfortunately, he wouldn't take the hint. By the time he left, my head was spinning.

Then I needed to go through the house and make sure it was presentable. That took longer than expected. There were still dirty dishes in the sink and crumbs on the table. The bed was unmade and the sheets were filthy. I did a load of laundry and changed the linens. When I looked up at the clock, it was nearing six. The sound of voices downstairs made my blood pressure rise. Time to greet Levi and the new Mrs. Wulf.

I couldn't believe my eyes. Levi had a baby in his arms.

"Samson. You remember Kya." He smiled broadly. "And this is my son." He shoved the squealing infant into my arms.

Levi looked so proud that I didn't have the heart to express my disapproval. "Congratulations. He's beautiful. He... he looks like you, Levi." The words were hollow, but it was the best I could do under the circumstances.

Levi didn't seem to notice, but Kya saw my discomfort and took the baby from my arms. "He's hungry."

I gave her a perfunctory hug.

Levi beamed. "Help me with the bags and the cradle while Kya feeds Junior."

Junior? Does he mean for this half-breed to be Alpha someday?

I followed him to the car. "Levi, we need to talk."

Levi had the good grace to look sheepish. "I know this is a shock, Samson, but Kya and I are meant to be together."

I shook my head. "Levi, she's a half-breed."

Levi's expression clouded in anger "Don't ever call her that again. She's as much a wolf as you or I."

I knew better than to argue with him. What good would it do anyway? What was done was done. "I'm sorry, Levi. I was thinking about your parents, and the rest of the pack."

"They'll come around. My wolf chose Kya. No one can argue with that. I called my father, and he admitted he made a mistake choosing Delilah for me. Lycan instinct overrides human prejudice. And if anyone objects, I'm prepared to take on any challengers." He paused. "Are you with me?"

I was disappointed that he'd doubted me. "Always."

"Good. I knew I could count on you." He clapped me on the back.

"There's just one thing, Levi. Delilah is still here and she overheard your message. She's very upset." I looked up at his parents' house. "She could be watching us as we speak."

Levi frowned. "I thought she'd gone home after I called off the wedding. I'll talk to her. Come with me. I don't want any trouble. First, let's take these things inside. Kya will want to put Junior down for a nap."

* * *

Levi knocked and his father came to the door. "Welcome home."

His mother came in from the kitchen. Hugs and kisses all around, and then they looked over our shoulders and said in unison, "Where's your son?"

I sighed. So typical of wolves to think of the child

and not the mother.

"All in good time." Levi said. "He's being fed."

I cleared my throat. "We need to see Delilah. She knows Levi is married and she's upset."

"Yes," Levi interjected. "I want to make peace before she goes home."

"It's the right thing to do," Rhona said. "I haven't seen her all day. She must be sulking in her room. I'll go fetch her."

We didn't have long to wait. Levi's mother rushed downstairs, a confused look on her face. "She's gone."

"What? Are you sure?" I asked.

"Yes. I looked in the closet. Her clothes are gone. Everything is gone."

Adrenaline flooded my body. *This is my fault. I should have gone to her sooner.* I wanted to run out of the house and look for her, but instead I remained where I was.

Levi snorted. "Well, that's just like her to run off without even a thank you. That bitch wants everyone to worry about her."

I couldn't keep the fear out of my voice. "Well, I'm worried."

Levi stood. "Don't be. Delilah can take care of herself. It's obvious she wants nothing to do with us. She's run home to Daddy so he can find her another sucker, er, mate. She'll be fine."

I wasn't so sure. "Excuse me. I'm going to call her and make sure she's all right." I stepped outside and called her cell phone, but it went right to voicemail. "This is Samson. I want to know that you're okay. Please call me as soon as you get this message."

When I returned, Levi's father had brought out a bottle of champagne. "Go get your family, Levi. We want to meet your bride. Samson, you'll stay and help us celebrate."

I was in no mood to celebrate, but there was nothing to do until I heard back from Delilah. "Yes, of course."

Levi returned with Kya and their sleeping baby. His parents gave Kya a quick hug, but they pounced on the baby, taking him out of the carrier and waking him up. He didn't cry and everyone marveled at his good nature.

Levi's father held him up in the air. "He's a Wulf for sure."

No one seemed concerned about Delilah. Except me.

Chapter Three

Samson

I called Delilah's phone several times during the night. Still no answer.

The next morning, I woke early and called again. Again, I got the voicemail. Levi could be right. She might not want to talk to any of us. Or she might still be sleeping.

My wolf didn't buy it. I had to know for sure.

I forced myself to wait fifteen minutes, and then I called again. *This is stupid.* I decided to call her father. I didn't have a number for him, so I had to call Levi. He wasn't happy to hear what I was up to. "Let it go," he said.

"I can't. You appointed me her caretaker, now I feel obligated to make sure she's okay."

"Oh, all right. Do what you feel is best."

I called her father immediately. "Alpha Ulric? Uh, this is Samson, beta of the Adirondack Pack. I'd like to speak to Delilah."

"What? Are you daft? Delilah is staying with your pack. Why are you calling me?"

My worst fears were realized and for a moment, I became speechless.

"Speak up. What's going on there?"

I had no choice. I had to tell him the truth. "Delilah left yesterday. We thought s-s-s-she was heading home."

"Well, you thought wrong. Are you sure she left? I spoke to her the other day and told her to stay put."

"Yes, S-S-S-Sir. She took all her clothes."

"Your pack is responsible for her well-being. Find her and keep her there until I arrive to pick her up." He hung up.

Where to start? With Levi, of course. I called him and told him what I'd learned.

He sounded worried when he responded. "Gather up the boys and start making phone calls. We need to have a meeting and find out if anyone saw her before she left."

* * *

Delilah

I pulled against my restraints. It was no use. I couldn't move. The covering over my head made it hard to breathe. *Where was I?* The cramped space, shifting motion, and sound of an engine told me that I was in the trunk of a car. How long? I had no idea. And there wasn't a damn thing I could do. I kept hoping it was just a cruel joke Bobby had engineered for payback.

Suddenly, all movement stopped. I went stiff when the trunk opened. *Maybe they'll let me go now.*

"Looks like she's still asleep."

"We'll see."

Someone pulled the sack off my head. I kept my eyes closed, but when I felt fingers pinch my cheek, I instinctively pulled my head back and opened my eyes.

"She's awake and dangerous. Knock her out again."

My ordeal wasn't over. I started squirming, screaming "No, no, no," but of course they couldn't hear me with my mouth taped shut.

The needle pricked my neck, and the hood covered my head again. The trunk slammed shut and the last thing I remembered was the engine starting up again.

* * *

Samson

Most of the pack crowded into the community room. There was a low rumble of conversation. People were curious. Levi didn't call meetings often. Axel and I sat up front with Levi and his parents.

"Where's Milo?" Levi whispered.

I shrugged. "Don't know. Axel tried calling him several times."

"Well, we can't wait. We'll start without him."

Levi stood. "Quiet." Silence fell over the room, and heads turned his way. "We have an emergency situation and I need everyone's attention."

I spotted Milo sneaking in. He slipped into a seat in the back. *He knows he belongs up front.* I rose to my feet. "Milo." His head jerked up. "Come up here and join us."

Milo cast a nasty look in my direction, but he stood. Adjusting his crotch, he walked up front and took a seat with us.

"Like I was saying," Levi continued speaking. "We have a problem. My ex-fiancée, Delilah Ulric, has gone missing."

A loud hubbub broke out. Levi's broken engagement wasn't public knowledge.

Levi held his arms up. "Quiet. Delilah's father, Max Ulric, Alpha of the Chicago Pack will be coming here to pick her up. Unfortunately, we have no idea where she is. We need to find her and make sure she's okay."

The clamor started again.

"If anyone saw her yesterday, I want to know."

Milo appeared to be thinking. A muscle twitched in his jaw and he shifted the ever-present fake cigarette from one side of his mouth to the other. He'd turned twenty-five a week ago, but he still acted like a kid. He loved attention and he thrived on trouble. He'd provoke it himself to stir up a little excitement. The expression on his face told me he knew something but he held his tongue.

Levi sounded desperate. "Surely someone saw her leave."

Milo cleared his throat and everyone turned to him. He avoided looking at Levi. "I might have seen her."

"What? Did you or didn't you?" My hands balled into fists as I stood over him.

Levi put a hand on my shoulder. "Sit down, Samson." He confronted Milo. "Well?"

"I saw her."

I stood again. "You're just now telling us this?"

Levi gave me a look. "All right, Milo. What happened?"

"She asked me not to tell anyone and I gave her my word."

"You're a fucking liar," I yelled.

Milo launched himself at me. His mouth was twisted with fury. I backed away, but things got ugly real fast. We circled each other and the pack went crazy, sensing a good fight. Milo balled his hands into fists, and swung at me. I blocked him, then came back with a punch to his gut. Milo doubled over and staggered backwards. He growled at me. "I'll kill you for this."

I growled back, "You can try." I got ready to swing again.

Levi came up behind me and caught me in a bear hug. "Enough," he shouted.

Milo took advantage of the opportunity to deliver a hard blow to my nose. Dazed, I shook my head back and forth, spraying blood in a wide arc.

Milo pulled his arm back for another punch, but Levi's father caught him before he could deliver. "You heard your Alpha. This pissing contest isn't helping us find Delilah."

Milo's ugly expression vanished. "You're right, sir. I'm sorry." He sat.

Ass kisser. Panting, I took my seat.

"Okay," Levi said. "Let's hear the whole story."

"Not much more to tell, Boss. She had a suitcase with her and she said she was going home. She planned to call a taxi from the main road. I told her Levi would never forgive me if I didn't give her a hand, and I offered her a lift to the train station. She said, on one condition. She didn't want Samson to know. Said he would raise an alarm and everyone would worry. I had to promise. I didn't want her waiting alone for a taxi, or hitching a ride with some stranger."

I spat at him. "You had no business keeping that promise."

Levi glared at me and I shut my mouth.

"Did you take her to the station?" Levi asked.

"I did."

"Did you wait until she got on the train?"

Milo looked sheepish as he shook his head.

Levi turned to me. "Okay, Samson, you're head of security. What's our next move?"

I thought fast. "I want to start at the train station. Maybe I can find out if she really bought a ticket for Chicago. If I'm lucky, I'll pick up a trail."

"Good idea. Take Milo and Axel with you."

"But, Alpha --"

Levi looked at me through narrowed eyes. "You heard me."

* * *

Delilah

I opened my eyes. Everything was dark and I couldn't move. Panic set in. *I'm buried alive.* A scream forced its way from deep inside me. *It's my worst nightmare.* My pulse quickened and I screamed again.

When I finally calmed down, I realized I was lying on a steel cot with a thin mattress. My wrists were chained to the headboard and my ankles to the footboard. My isolation was total. No sound, no light. I could have been anywhere. I looked for a window. There was none, just a steel door leading to what?

Disoriented, I had no clue how much time had passed, or if it was night or day. I would go mad in here. I stared at the door, almost willing it to open. Eventually it did. A tall, smiling man entered and walked toward me. With his broad shoulders, black hair, and chiseled features, he was the living embodiment of tall, dark and handsome, but I saw evil in his cold gray eyes.

"Hello, pet. I thought you might be awake by now. You're probably thirsty. Hungry, too. Answer my questions and I'll feed you."

I tried to sit, but my wrists refused to move. The cuffs dug into my skin. "Who are you?"

"I ask the questions here. What's your name?"

I didn't respond.

"It doesn't matter. You'll be getting a new one."

I felt cold, icy anger. My nostrils flared. My lips drew back and fangs broke through my gums. I snarled. Everything in me screamed attack, but of course that was impossible.

A big grin creased his face. "Wonderful. You've shown me your true colors."

Damn it. Inside I cursed myself for letting him get to me.

"I was told you're a shifter, but I had to see for myself. Thank you for providing the proof I needed. And that brings us to the reason you're here. Selective breeding."

My blood went cold. I knew there were humans who hunted us for their own purposes. It was the reason we lived in our own communities and played human when we entered theirs.

"It's the process of breeding animals for particular traits."

I spat at him. "I know what it means."

"Of course you do. You're not just a dumb animal. You're domesticated. But let me explain how this will work. First, you'll be thoroughly examined and we'll need to do a DNA study. Then you'll be matched with compatible human males. I hope to be the first, but we'll have to wait for the tests. After all, indiscriminate breeding could result in poor quality. And as much as I look forward to fucking you, in the end, this is all about the money, so everything will be done scientifically." He squeezed my leg. "But don't worry. I'll make it fun for you. If you cooperate, that is."

"I won't do it."

"You have no choice."

"Bastard."

"You'll call me Sir from now on."

"I'll call you whatever I damn well please."

"I like your spunk. I'm almost sorry I have to break you."

"I'll never break."

"It may take time, but you *will* break. And when you do, I'll make things more comfortable for you. A nice room. Good meals."

"I don't care about those things."

He shrugged. "You will."

Chapter Four

Sampson

We weren't sure Delilah had gotten on the train, so I asked Milo and Axel to search the area. Milo looked at me with suspicion. "What are you going to do?"

"Follow a hunch. I'm taking the train to Penn Station."

"Why?" Axel asked.

"If Delilah wanted to disappear, what better place than Manhattan? Maybe I'll pick up her scent."

"We'll go with you," Milo said.

"No. This area needs to be searched. I'll call you and let you know what I find." The men weren't happy, and I turned away before they could protest.

* * *

I usually drove to New York. This was my first time on the train. We traveled through some of Upstate New York's most picturesque regions, but I couldn't enjoy any of it. I spent every second worrying about Delilah and sniffing around for her scent.

I reached Penn Station without detecting a trace of Delilah. The underground labyrinth was a challenging place to navigate, but I kept my nose attuned to Delilah's scent. It was already hardwired into my brain and my sense of smell is one hundred times more sensitive than a human's. Even so, I was shocked to find traces of Delilah everywhere. She must have gotten lost and wandered through the maze of tunnels until she found her way out.

My pulse picked up when I followed her trail up a set of steps to the sidewalks of New York. I let my nose lead me through the doors of the Renaissance Hotel. The desk clerk remembered a tall, beautiful redhead who asked about a room, but never checked in. "She seemed put off by the rate."

I thanked him and left. Obviously, Delilah was being frugal with her money. I spent the better part of an hour questioning hotel clerks and finally a hostel. It looked like a dump and although I was anxious to find Delilah, I half hoped that she hadn't ended up here.

The young man at the desk was leaning over a computer game on his phone. His long, greasy hair covered his face. I cleared my throat three times before he looked up. "Yeah?"

He flipped his hair back and I did a double take. He had stitches along the side of his face. It looked like claw marks. I was sure Delilah must have put them there. A surge of anger made my blood run hot. *What did you do to my* -- I tamped down my rage. Delilah wasn't mine, and if I threatened this asshole he wouldn't tell me anything.

On the outside, I remained calm. On the inside, my wolf was a mass of howling rage. "I need a room for one night."

"You're in luck. One opened up on the third floor. You have to share the bath."

"I'll take it."

"Fifty bucks. Cash, and in advance."

He took my money, stuffed it in his pocket and handed me a key. "The elevators aren't working. Fire stairs are to your left."

I nodded and took the stairs two at a time, following Delilah's scent down the hall to her room. She had definitely been here and her scent was still fresh. But where the hell was she now? My wolf growled at her familiar smell, wanting to find her and mark her. Claiming her was not an option, but my wolf was too near the surface, and hard to control.

Needing to focus, I tamped my feelings down and followed her scent to the bathroom. Delilah's unique scent had left the smell of fear all over the small bathroom. She hadn't left willingly. Someone had taken her.

I blamed myself. I was supposed to keep her safe while Levi was gone. Instead, I'd been lax, allowing her to hear Levi's message and doing nothing to calm her down. I'd thought I could handle her and all my other shit at the same time, but I'd let her slip through my fingers. I had no idea of who'd taken her, but I knew it involved the asshole at the front desk.

I went back to her room, sat down, and put my head in my hands. I was usually in control, but not this time. Somewhere along the way, I'd fallen for my best friend's girl and lost it. Guilt hammered at me, making it difficult to come up with a plan. *Think, damn it.*

She was a missing person, but I couldn't go to the police. I knew for a fact shifters were kidnapped by shady corporations for research or sex trafficking every day. Corrupt cops often worked with them. And if I didn't mention Delilah was a she-wolf, the cops wouldn't be able to narrow their suspects down to a workable list. I'd be better off doing this on my own. But I needed to hurry. Kidnappers could be flying her overseas at that very moment.

The desk clerk -- nametag read "Bobby" -- must have fingered her for somebody. But who? At any rate, he knew something. I had to find out, but I had to be careful, too. Bobby Boy might sic his thug friends on me and then I'd lose any chance of rescuing Delilah.

I tried to think of my next move, but my mind kept straying. Every time I thought of Delilah, my heart ached. She was gorgeous, a real spitfire, yet still so innocent. I'd never met anyone like her and I couldn't imagine my world without her. And yet, it might come to that. There were too many people who would exploit our unique species for their own profit. What were those fucking bastards doing to her? I was going mad thinking about it.

Enraged, I started pacing, trying to figure out what to do. Finally, a light bulb went off. A plan formed in my mind. I would need Bobby Boy's help, but it shouldn't be hard to convince him helping me was in his best interests.

* * *

Delilah

I woke up to find my restraints were gone. There was only a cuff on my ankle that chained me to the bed. I was dizzy, but I sat up and let my head clear before I stood. The chain rattled with every step as I walked the short distance to the stainless-steel toilet. I did my business and walked around the perimeter of my cell. When I got to the door, I pounded on it. It was solid steel and I doubted that anyone had heard me. Back at the bed, I sank down in despair.

Claustrophobia was my curse. I prized my freedom above all else. My kind weren't meant to be caged. In here, I felt the walls closing in on me. I couldn't breathe. I needed to see the trees, to feel the sun on my face, and smell the flowers. My heart ached for freedom and open spaces. When I was outdoors, all was right with my world.

I tried to think of ways to escape, but my fear grew into all out panic. Terrified and exhausted, I prayed to Fenrir, the Lord of Wolves. "Please help me. I beg you. Let me leave this dark hole and I promise I'll leave New York forever. I'll go home and help my father protect our pack from human predators."

I fell into a fitful sleep and when I woke, a strange man in a white coat was standing over the bed watching me. "Who are you?"

"I'm the doctor. Today I'm going to do a quick preliminary exam. If everything looks good we'll move you to the clinic for further tests."

The doctor stood tall and straight like a soldier. His face didn't give a clue as to what he was thinking. Behind his glasses, his eyes were cold and humorless. Yet this man might be my only hope. He was a doctor, after all. He was supposed to help people.

A Neanderthal in scrubs stood at the door holding a gun. It was pointed at me. I stared at it and gripped my scratchy blanket.

The doctor followed my gaze and reassured me. "If you behave, there's no need to worry. It's just loaded with tranquilizer darts."

Bad enough. I'm going to behave. I didn't want to be knocked out again. I wanted to talk to the doctor and gain his confidence. Fenrir would forgive me for lying. "Doctor, you've got to help me get home. I take a special medicine. If I don't have it I can't control my beast."

He studied me in a distant way. "It sounds like a tranquilizer. I can help you with that."

My voice rose and cracked into a sob. "No, no. It's something else. Something only my father has."

"Calm down." He looked over at the Neanderthal and the bearded man approached.

"I don't need a tranquilizer."

He waved away the guard. "I'll make those decisions. Now do as I say or I'll have to put you to sleep."

I nodded and the doctor took my blood pressure and temperature. He listened to my heart. His hands were cold as he checked every part of my body.

"Now I'm going to check the size and shape of your uterus and ovaries. Raise your knees and spread your legs."

I shook my head vigorously. "No!"

The Neanderthal pointed his weapon at me and I did as I was told. I closed my eyes and gritted my teeth as the doctor inserted two lubricated, gloved fingers into my vagina. His other hand pressed on the outside of my lower abdomen.

When the prodding was over I opened my eyes in the hope of speaking to him again, but it was the Neanderthal standing over me. The doctor removed his gloves and tossed them into the sink.

"Doctor, please?"

But he was already out the door. The guard followed him and I started to cry. Now I felt even more alone.

* * *

Samson

It only took a little chat -- and a shapeshift -- to convince Bobby that it would be in his best interests to help me rescue Delilah. There was just one hitch. The wolf traffickers were looking for females.

"They think she-wolves will be easier to control and they want to breed them with humans."

I wanted to punch out his lights. "And you thought it would be a good idea to help them?"

The asshole flinched. "I needed the money." He actually started to cry. "I'm helping you now, aren't I?"

I didn't trust him as far as I could toss him. I intended to keep Bobby on a short leash from now on. I knew he'd run to the kidnappers if he had the chance. "Keep your mouth shut and stick close, and I won't kill you."

"I will. I swear it."

I showed him my fangs and he sat on the bed like a good boy. Then I went out to the hallway to make my call. Axel and Milo agreed with my plan. Milo was a jealous adversary, but he would do anything to save one of his own kind. He hated humans as much as I did and he was the kind of fierce, formidable wolf you wanted on your side when you're fighting them. I asked him to call Levi and relay the plan.

Levi had no love for Delilah, and he wouldn't want to put one of our females at risk, but he had no choice. One of our women would have to be the decoy. I knew Levi would come through. This was his chance to show his true colors and be the brave, caring Alpha I knew he was.

* * *

Samson

I sat in the lobby and kept an eagle eye on Bobby while he worked his shift. Then we went upstairs and waited in Delilah's room. Being cooped up with that little shit was no fun, but I had no choice. I needed him to put my plan in motion, and I couldn't leave him alone. We ended up spending the night together, Bobby on the bed, me on the floor -- in my wolf fur. I don't think Bobby closed his eyes all night.

The next day, we went out to breakfast, but I couldn't swallow a bite. When we came back, I started pacing. I must have walked miles, enough to wear a path in the thin carpet. I was so lost in going over my plan that at first I didn't hear the knock at the door. When I opened it, Levi walked in with Milo, Axel, and three more of our biggest wolves. I thought Bobby would shit himself. I almost did, too, when Kya stepped out from behind them. I was shocked. My gaze shifted from her to Levi.

Levi's face was drawn and tense. "She insisted," he said, grimly.

Kya took his arm and looked up at him lovingly. "I have to do this for Delilah. I know she hates me and I want to make things right between us."

Maybe Levi is right after all. Kya is one of us. "She'll be grateful," I said. "So am I. It's very brave of you."

From the corner of my eye, I saw Levi studying Bobby. "Is that the traitor?"

Bobby wrapped his arms around himself and glanced up nervously at Levi.

"Yes, he's going to make the phone call that will put our plan into action."

Levi's voice was edged with burnished steel. "Let's get on with it."

I gave Bobby his phone, but before he could make the call I had to calm him down. He was so frightened that I didn't think he'd sound natural.

He took a few deep breaths and punched in the number. "Yes, yes, it's Bobby. Sorry, boss. I didn't mean to bother you, but I got a good lead here. The redhead's friend showed up. They were supposed to meet. And she's one hot piece of ass."

I thought Levi would blow a gasket. Kya put a hand on his arm, and her soothing touch calmed him. He managed to keep his hands off Bobby.

Bobby looked scared but he kept talking. "Yeah, yeah. Even better-looking than the last one." He was quiet for a moment. "I'm not working that shift. Okay. I'll leave an envelope with the key for you." He hung up. "How did I do?"

"Not bad," I said. "Now if all goes well, you'll

get to live."

Later, one of the guys went out for food. We sat on the floor and went over the plan while we ate. Afterward we went next door and left Levi and Kya alone to say their goodbyes. When Levi joined us, he looked troubled. I knew he was worried about Kya. He sat on the floor, a muscle twitching at his jaw. Then he leaned his head against the wall so he could hear every move she made.

Suddenly I was filled with doubts. Were we doing the right thing? We could lose both Kya and Delilah. Part of me said to call it off. The other part knew this was the only chance to save Delilah. Dread and indecision tied my stomach in knots. I sat wide-awake, and chewing on my nails. Time passed slowly. I closed my eyes, intending to rest them for just a minute.

* * *

Something jarred me awake and I bolted up. Axel was shaking me. "Get ready," he mouthed.

I came fully awake and nodded. I tied up Bobby and covered his mouth with duct tape.

Levi was listening at the wall. Sweat glistened on his forehead and his hands were clenched into fists. I'd never seen him so distraught. White-lipped and grim, he turned to us. "It's done," he said, in a flat, resigned voice. "They've taken her."

"Not for long," I told him.

We left the hotel quickly, in time to see two men locking the trunk of a dark sedan and preparing to drive away. Our two cars trailed them at a safe distance.

The sedan led us to Brooklyn. I smelled the polluted canal before I saw it. The black car drove to a deserted area and pulled over at an abandoned building. We parked nearby and got out of our cars. Moving silently, we came up behind the kidnappers as they were taking Kya from the trunk. The element of surprise was with us. The two thugs were docile as sheep. I took their weapons while Axel cuffed their wrists in front of them. Levi made sure Kya was okay. She appeared frightened but refused to wait in the car.

Shifters don't have the time or patience for modesty. We're in and out of our clothes all the time. I don't think Kya gave a damn about modesty either since she'd been a stripper when we met. But Levi wasn't having it. "Okay, Kya, but you're not going in like that. Wait here. I'll get you something to wear from the car."

"No!"

We all looked at Kya in surprise. Even the thugs seemed shocked into silence.

"It hurts!" She let out a bloodcurdling scream.

We circled her and watched as she dropped to the ground. Parts of her body bulged and then shrunk, as if something was alive inside her. Black fur crept over her flesh. In a matter of minutes, a black wolf lay there, panting. Kya rolled over and showed her belly to her dominant partner. Levi crouched by her side and nuzzled her. I could swear he had tears in his eyes, but I'd never have said it out loud.

Good for you, Kya. I'd had no idea that demiwolves could shift. If Kya wanted to prove she was one of us, she couldn't have chosen a better way.

Levi stood. "Let's get moving."

Kya obeyed immediately. She leaped to her paws and growled at her abductors. I helped Levi push the thugs forward, cautioning them to keep their mouths shut. One of them punched a code into the keypad by the door and it opened. We entered a foyer and a watchman came forward, looking confused. It took him a minute to realize their hideaway had been breached. He reached for a weapon, but Kya lunged at him and knocked him down. One of our men tied him up and dragged him behind a desk. Levi took his gun. He pointed it at Kya's kidnappers and urged them on. "No tricks or you're dead men."

They led us to a service elevator and we took it to the basement. The doors opened and another man stood there waiting.

"What took you guys so long? I've been --"

We pushed the two thugs into the third guy, and all three went down. Levi brandished his gun. "Get on your feet, scumbags. We want our female back. Lead the way."

With a wolf and a gun at their backs, they led us down a concrete hall and came to a stop in front of a steel door.

"Hurry up," I yelled, anxious to set eyes on Delilah. I couldn't believe she'd been forced to stay in this cement hell.

One of the creeps pulled out a set of keys and started to open the door.

I heard gunshots behind me. "Come on. Unlock the Goddamn door."

He turned the key, but the gunfire sounded closer. Our men grabbed the thugs and used them as human shields. More shots rang out and the shields went limp. They slid to the floor. Levi shoved the bodies aside and I heard his bones creaking as he started changing. The others followed suit and charged the shooter.

I opened the door of the cell and Kya slipped through. I followed her. Delilah sat on the bed, wrapped in a threadbare blanket. She looked so small and helpless and she'd been crying. I'd never seen her like that. It made my heart ache. I sat beside her and put an arm around her. "You're safe now."

She opened her mouth and seemed about to answer me, then her nostrils flared and she turned to the black she-wolf. "What is this?"

"This is your savior."

Delilah bared her teeth. "She stinks of Levi. This is his half-breed whore."

We recognize our own by chemical signature and Kya's was unmistakable. "She's one of us, Delilah. None of this is her fault, but she insisted on coming here to rescue you."

"I didn't ask for her help, and I don't want it."

I hoped Delilah would change her mind, but this wasn't the time to fix things between the she-wolves. Kya padded softly out of the cell. I sighed and turned to Delilah. "We'll talk about it later. Right now we need to get you out of here."

The keys were still in the door. I tried them all until I found one that fit the cuff on Delilah's ankle. The shackle had left an angry bruise on her flesh. I touched it gently and she winced, but didn't complain. When I tried to pick her up, she resisted.

"You've been through an ordeal," I told her. "Let me help you."

"I can walk on my own."

She was stubborn, a real spitfire. Maybe that was the attraction. I didn't mind taking orders, especially from her. "Okay. You'll heal faster if you shift. And stay close. I'll lead you out to the car."

* * *

Delilah

I tried to shift, but nothing happened. Something

- 110 -

held me back. It had to be the drugs they'd been injecting me with. Focusing on my wolf, I tried harder. Still nothing.

I thought about my kidnappers, what my wolf could do to them, and suddenly I felt the change coming. I pictured my powerful jaws and sharp fangs tearing those men to shreds. I could almost taste their blood and feel their terror.

My heart started racing. My pulse sped up. My bones broke and twisted like matchsticks. I went to all fours, and rolled my head around until my neck snapped. My jaw stretched into a muzzle. Fur spread over my body and I started to lick my thick auburn coat. I knew I looked good. The proof was in Samson's eyes. He stared at me as if I were a goddess. It proved what I already knew. He had a crush on me. I liked him, too, but the differences between us were insurmountable.

Samson followed my lead and morphed into a gorgeous wolf with a rich tawny brown pelt. It looked so soft, I wanted to nuzzle him, but I shook it off. I wanted blood more, and I took off before he could stop me.

I ran through the hall, Samson at my heels, and threw myself into the fray. Two men were cornering Kya. One had a gun. Without thinking, I lunged. He struggled under my weight, but he was no match for me. I crushed his throat with my jaws. Kya tackled his partner. Her prey hit the floor. She crouched over him and finished him off.

I looked around. Samson had joined the fight. The men had things well under control. Kya barked her thanks, and I let her lead me outside.

We shifted and dressed in the sweats we found in the car and Kya told me her story. I didn't mind listening now that I'd repaid my debt. I'd never liked owing anyone, especially not a demiwolf. I had to admit she'd had a rough life, and I respected her bravery. "You proved yourself today, Kya. Thank you."

"Thank *you*, Delilah."

I raised a brow. "Why thank me?"

"You were the catalyst that caused my change. Until today I was never sure I had it in me."

Her words had an impact on me. Maybe I'd misjudged her. "You acted like a true she-wolf and a loyal member of the pack. Everyone will have to accept you now."

"Do you accept me, Delilah?"

I thought for a moment. "Yes. You saved me from a life of hell. When you get tired of that jerk you married, there's a place for you in my pack."

Her eyes went wide. Her mouth opened. And we both busted out laughing.

That's how the men found us when they came out of the building.

* * *

Samson

Delilah and Kya appeared to be hitting it off. I was curious and wanted to know how they'd resolved their issues, but I couldn't get near them. Levi climbed into their SUV along with some of the others and I was forced to ride in the second vehicle.

We arrived back home and Levi's mother fixed us a meal. Delilah related what she'd been through and all the talk revolved around retaliation.

"They're all dead," Levi said. "Who do you want to retaliate against?"

"Bobby," I blurted out.

"He doesn't know anything, and he's scared shitless. There's nothing to fear from him. Besides if we let him live, he might lead us to others who are higher up in the organization."

Levi's father spoke. "Those higher ups might kill him for us."

"We don't even know if there are any others. All we can do now is tighten security and watch our backs."

I had to agree with Levi. We needed to prepare for trouble in the future.

Someone asked Delilah about her plans. My ears perked up. Now that was something I wanted to know.

"I called my father and told him I wanted to come home. He insisted on coming to get me and I refused his offer. I'm not a baby who needs her daddy to pick her up. Of course we had a fight, but I let him win. When I was locked in that cell, I made a promise to Fenrir that I would be a good daughter, and I intend to keep it."

It was a stab in my heart. I knew it was coming, but hearing her say it made it real. I couldn't celebrate her leaving. I just wanted to be alone. After dinner I wandered outside and went for a walk.

The woods at dusk were paradise, a quiet place where I liked to think. I took a path that led into the depths of the forest. My senses opened up to the smell of vegetation and the sounds of small animals running from my scent.

I finally admitted to myself that I loved Delilah. But I couldn't do a damn thing about it. Everyone would laugh if they knew, especially Delilah. She was a formidable woman, daughter of an Alpha, and meant to wed a strong Alpha who could control her, not a beta like me. Even if we could overcome our differences, she was my best friend's ex. There was no way we could mate and live in close proximity to Levi and Kya.

In my heart, I felt we could be a good match, but she would never know. The darkness increased and a sense of isolation came over me. Resigned, I turned and headed home.

Chapter Five

Delilah

After dinner, I looked for Samson. I wanted to thank him personally for coming to my rescue, but he was gone. Disappointed, I pleaded exhaustion and everyone agreed that we should call it a night.

My suitcase and phone were gone only God knew where, so Kya went next door and brought me back some clothes. They weren't my usual style, but beggars can't be choosers. I was lucky to be alive.

I sprawled across the bed, but had trouble falling asleep. Something nagged at me, a sense of impending doom. "You're safe." I kept repeating it, but it didn't help.

A knock sounded at the door. I sat up and turned on the light. "Come in."

Levi's parents entered the room. His mother looked like she'd been crying and fear clutched at my heart. They sat on the bed, one on either side of me.

Rhona put her arm around me. "Oh, Delilah. I'm so sorry."

My blood turned to ice as I looked from one to the other.

Levi's father sighed. "There's no easy way to say this, Delilah. Your father passed on. He died of a massive heart attack."

"Oh my God." I swallowed a sob that rose in my throat. "I have to talk to my mother."

"She's resting now. Your pack doctor gave her a sedative. He was the one who called me."

Rhona hugged me. "Go on now. Cry. You don't have to be strong for us."

I let myself weep aloud, and I rocked back and forth like a child while Rhona held me. Finally, I composed myself. "I need to go home as soon as possible."

"I know, child," the old Alpha comforted me. "Try to get some rest, and I'll find someone to take you home in the morning."

"Thank you."

Rhona tucked me in. "Call me if you need anything. I'll be right down the hall."

I said I would, but I knew I wouldn't. The only thing I needed was to get home. I felt responsible for my father's death and overwhelmed with guilty thoughts about the stress I'd caused him. I'd known he was aging, but I'd only been concerned with my independence. Why hadn't I been a better daughter? All the shoulda, woulda, couldas in the world wouldn't bring him back. All I could do now was step up, and be the daughter he'd deserved.

I was a girl on a mission, finally getting a sense of who I really was. In this time of chaos, I felt a calm I never knew before. My mind was clear. I was in my element, in command of my life, and ready to fulfill my destiny.

* * *

Samson

I didn't expect a thank you or a goodbye from Delilah, so when she called me early the next morning, I was shocked. "G-g-good m-m-morning, Delilah."

"Samson, I'm sure you're probably sick of being forced to look out for me, but something's come up and I need your help."

Her voice sounded huskier than normal, like she'd been crying. Whatever happened, I was just glad she was coming to me. "Anything. Just name it."

"My father died last night. A heart attack. I need

to get home."

While I'd been out in the woods, feeling sorry for myself, Delilah had been dealing with her father's death. I felt like a selfish bastard. "Oh my God, I'm so sorry. What can I do?"

"Take me home. My mother is lost. I need to be with her."

"Of course."

"There's one little problem. Levi's father asked Milo to drive me to Chicago. He feels that driving would be safer than taking public transportation." She hesitated for a moment. "I don't entirely trust Milo. He's a player and I don't want to spend all that time alone with him."

Suddenly happy, I smiled inside. "You can trust me, Delilah. I'll sort it out."

"I'm so relieved. Let's leave as soon as possible. Oh, and Samson…"

"Yes."

"Pack a small bag. I'd like you to stay for the funeral. You can represent your pack."

It wasn't a declaration of love, by any means, but she needed me and that was enough. As soon as we hung up, I called Levi's father and told him I'd be driving Delilah home. He didn't sound happy. He'd probably guessed how I felt about her and had wanted to keep us apart. The man was old, but he wasn't stupid. He knew how to read people and I'd always had trouble hiding my feelings. But he didn't protest, so I hung up and called Milo. I told him that the plan had changed and his services were no longer required.

His response was, "Fucker." And he hung up on me.

Same to you, buddy. I packed some clothes in a duffle bag and threw it in the back of my old Subaru.

Then I left to pick up Delilah. She was waiting outside with Levi's parents. His father told me to take care of her and I said I would. Delilah didn't have much to bring home, just a small tote with a few things she'd borrowed from Kya. I put her bag with mine and we climbed inside in the car. Alone in close quarters, I suddenly felt shy. I wanted to break the awkward silence. Guess she did, too. We both started talking at once. "What did you --"

"Why are you --"

We looked at each other for a second, and then started laughing, but it broke the ice. "Ladies first."

"I was just wondering what you said to Levi's father. He seemed a bit cold when we said our goodbyes."

"He'll get over it. He's used to getting his way, but in this case he made a mistake."

Delilah chuckled. "I'm sure he just wanted to give you a break from being my babysitter."

"I don't want to be your babysitter." I took my eyes off the road to look at Delilah. We made eye contact at exactly the same time and the connection was so powerful, I forgot where I was. I thought of all the dirty things I wanted to do to her.

"Watch out!"

Delilah grabbed the wheel and steered us back to our lane. I'd narrowly missed a head-on with an eighteen-wheeler. I took in a deep breath and steadied myself. "S-s-s-sorry."

"No harm done. So, you don't want to be my babysitter. What do you want?"

I want to be your lover, your mate, your partner. "I want to be your friend."

"You are my friend, Samson. You're the only one I trust to get me home. Milo just wants to fuck me."

I felt my face grow hot. I'd just been thinking the same thing. She was just so damn gorgeous, so tempting. But unlike Milo, I would never hit on her. "Well, you don't have to worry about that with me."

* * *

Delilah

Too bad. "Yes, you're a perfect gentleman." Despite my independence, I'd had little experience with men. She-wolves were supposed to wait for marriage and I'd been promised to an Alpha. In the past, I'd been tempted to have sex just to spite my father, but I'd never met anyone I deemed worthy of taking my virginity. Until now.

Why did it have to be a beta who woke butterflies in my stomach? He stared at me as if he wanted to eat me alive, and it was hot as hell. His scent, all male and oh so seductive, made me drool. Amazing. I only drooled when I smelled the scent of a fresh kill. I love deer meat. It really surprised me that I'd succumbed so easily to Samson's powerful sexuality. I don't think he realized how delicious he was. He had the kind of body that any woman would appreciate. That thought gave me pause. I didn't want to think of him with someone else. I wanted him all to myself. I wanted my first time to be with him. Images of our naked bodies grinding together in passion flitted through my mind.

I gave myself a mental shake and tried to stop thinking about sex. I had other things to worry about, like staying alive and taking over the pack when I got home. But my head was between the sheets. It must be my wolf, frustrated and ready to mate. Well, the randy beast would not get its way. Samson was a pretty piece of eye candy, and tempting as hell, but he was a beta.

Still, I had to force myself to stop looking at him. Closing my eyes, I pretended to be asleep. Soon, I didn't have to pretend. The motion of the car made me drowsy. My eyes felt heavy. A long car ride could be a boring undertaking, but I looked forward to some spicy dreams.

Chapter Six

Delilah

Someone shook me, and I came awake with a start, all flailing arms and snapping jaws. Strong arms grabbed me and held me close, but I struggled to get away.

"Calm down, little spitfire. You're safe. I've got you."

I looked into Samson's eyes and I did feel safe. For a second, I thought he was going to kiss me. Then he backed off.

"You were agitated, talking in your sleep. I pulled into this parking lot to wake you."

So much for sexy dreams. "It was a nightmare. I was back in that horrid cell." I shuddered. "I thought the doctor was putting his hands on me again. Did you kill him, Samson? He wore a white coat and glasses."

"I didn't see anyone with a white coat. Maybe he took it off."

"I hate him. I hope he's dead."

"He'll never hurt you again. If he's still alive, I'll find him and finish him off."

I broke down, weeping bitterly. "I'm sorry. I want to be strong, but sometimes it's just too much. Oh, God. I just want to forget it ever happened."

"I'll try to distract you." Samson stopped short and turned as red as my hair. "I mean…"

I forced a smile. "It's okay. I get it."

He breathed a sigh of relief. "We've been driving for hours. I can get us a room at this motel." He pointed at the building across the lot. "I think you'll be safer sleeping with me." He cleared his throat, and then added quickly, "Two beds, of course."

"Of course," I agreed. "Let's do it. I'm exhausted

and I could use a shower."

Samson checked us in. Our room was in the inner courtyard, hidden from the road. Adequate described it best. It was dingy and there were mysterious stains on the carpet, but at least it had two queen-size beds and it was clean. It smelled of bleach.

"I'm going to take a shower." I disappeared into the bathroom and shut the door. I leaned against it and breathed a sigh of relief. It was so hard to be around him when all I wanted to do was touch him. Samson was a man of contradictions, sometimes sweet and shy, sometimes bursting with primal intensity. Both Samsons gave me a fluttery feeling in my belly. I liked that feeling very much, but it was diverting me from my purpose.

Sexual desire could be a dangerous distraction. I had to ignore it, no matter how good it made me feel.

A cold shower might do the trick. I let the icy stream pour over me, but it didn't stop the sexy thoughts racing through my brain. Part of me wanted to shout, "Come in here and share my shower." The other part scolded me. "What are you thinking? This man is a beta. Worse, he's the type to get all serious." But I couldn't stop thinking about him and what it might feel like to have him inside me.

I kept wishing his tall, muscular frame stood beside me in the shower. I wanted to look up into those dark, heavy-lidded eyes and kiss his soft, sexy lips. Every detail of his face haunted me. In the car, the air had seemed to sizzle between us. Every time we were together, our connection grew stronger. I could tell that he was struggling for control just as I was.

I sighed and shut off the water. I couldn't stay in here forever. I put on sweat pants and a T-shirt, and left the bathroom.

* * *

Samson

"My turn." I practically ran into the bathroom and shut the door. Delilah looked so adorable, almost childlike with her wet hair wrapped in a towel and no makeup. Her skin glowed from the shower, and her eyes shone like green glass. But she was no child. Her big breasts jiggled temptingly under her white T-shirt and she gave me an encouraging look. I wanted to kiss her so bad, but instead I ran away.

Why am I acting so fucking wimpy? Because I am a wimp. Levi is the Alpha and I'm the beta. He'd gone after what he wanted, consequences be damned. That wasn't me, especially when it involved the Alpha's ex. My timidity around women insured I didn't have much romance in my life. Maybe I should change my tactics, try to be more like Levi, just hop into her bed and shower her with kisses. But I knew I couldn't do it.

I turned up the hot water and stepped under the stream. I soaped up, rinsed, dried off, brushed my teeth, combed my hair, and applied deodorant and cologne. Just in case. Then I wrapped a towel around my waist and opened the door.

Delilah was lying on the bed with her eyes closed. *Damn.* She rolled over and let out a shaky little breath. What had I been thinking? She was scared and traumatized and all I could think about was fucking her. She needed to sleep more than anything. I plopped down on the other bed. I might as well get some sleep, too.

* * *

Something woke me. I opened my eyes and saw Delilah pacing around the room. Immediately alert, I jumped out of bed and went to her. "What's wrong?

Did you hear something?"

"Stop crowding me like a mama wolf. I'm not a pup."

I was hurt, but not surprised. "I know that."

"So does your dick. It's stabbing my belly."

I jumped back. I'd known she had a sharp tongue, but I'd never heard the word dick come out of her mouth. It shocked me and excited me at the same time. "S-s-s-sorry. You're a beautiful woman."

She started crying.

"I didn't mean to make you cry."

"I'm the one who's sorry. It's not you. I'm just confused and scared. I've never been scared in my whole life and I hate it."

"Everyone is scared at some point."

"Not you."

"Yeah, me. I was scared to talk when I was a kid. The boys bullied me when I stuttered. But I got over it. And you'll get over this."

Delilah gave me a curious look. "But sometimes you still stutter."

"Only around you. You make me nervous."

"I don't mean to."

"I know." I didn't want to talk about my stutter anymore. "Let's get you back to bed." I drew her toward her bed and she climbed under the covers. "We'll talk more in the morning."

Before I could walk away, she grabbed my hand and pulled me down. "Sleep with me? I'll feel safer if you do." How could I refuse? I slid in next to her. "Thank you, Samson. For telling me that story." She melted into my arms and gave me a goodnight kiss.

I wanted more, but she turned her back, prepared to go to sleep. I spooned her, my dick settling along the crease of her ass, but she didn't seem bothered. In fact, she sighed and pressed closer. My presence seemed to comfort her. In a few moments, I heard her steady breathing and assumed she was asleep.

I, on the other hand, was wide-awake. How could I sleep with Delilah's enticing scent all around me? I couldn't help burying my nose against her neck and inhaling. My restless wolf went wild and I nuzzled her relentlessly.

After a few moments, Delilah turned in my arms, placed her nose at my throat and sniffed in my scent.

"I didn't mean to wake you."

She murmured against my skin. "It's the way of the wolf. She's so wound up, so hot and horny…" Delilah moaned. "I can't fight her. I bend to her will."

"Oh fuck. My little spitfire."

* * *

Delilah

Samson's voice sounded husky with emotion and lust. Our breaths mingled and he captured my lips in an eager kiss. It was magic. His mouth was warmer and softer than I'd imagined. Moaning, I opened my mouth and his tongue slipped inside. That kiss set me on fire and I couldn't think straight. I slipped out of his grasp to remove my clothes.

"Oh, God. Delilah. You're so beautiful."

My heart fluttered at the way he whispered my name. His warm body against my naked flesh felt so perfect, so right; instinctively I started grinding against him. A growl rumbled up from his chest and he rolled to his back, pulling me with him. My wolf knew what he wanted, what we both wanted. Straddling his hips, I rose on my knees and guided his cock to my weeping pussy.

Samson gripped my hips, stopping me before I could go any further.

"Are you sure, Spitfire? Is this what you want?"

My wolf was sure. Our animal spirits shared an overwhelming desire to fuck. That meant something in my world. "It's what my wolf wants."

"And mine." He sighed and let me go.

A rhythmic pulse beat in my pussy, an ache to be filled. Positioning myself over his stiff cock, I slid down slowly. I was wet, but there was still pain. "Ohh…"

Samson froze. "Are you okay?"

"I will be. Touch me."

Samson reached up and caressed my breasts. He teased my nipples and every tug went straight to my dripping pussy. At last, his cock was fully inside me, and pleasure overrode the pain. I whimpered with joy. "You feel so good."

Samson groaned. "Yes. So good. So fucking tight. Ride me, Spitfire."

I slid up and down on his shaft, slowly, then faster, as I lost myself in animal heat.

"Oh, yes, that's it, baby." He gripped my hips and moved me up and down on his cock.

I caught the rhythm and he let his hands roam my body. I reveled in his touch, the feel of him inside me. Savage animal sounds echoed in the room, and I realized they were coming from me. Lost in a place of primal sensation, I couldn't think, I could only feel.

Samson teased my clit and my muscles contracted around him, making him growl. He bucked his hips up, driving deeper inside me and filling me with load after load of hot cum. His climax triggered my orgasm. Ecstatic, I screamed out his name again and again.

He pulled me down and I didn't realize what he was doing until his teeth sank into my flesh. I screamed at the pain and Samson licked the wound, where my neck met my shoulder. In an instant, the pain was replaced by more pleasure. At last, I opened my eyes and looked into his.

"Are you okay, baby?"

Samson's cock was still hard inside me and I was lost in post-orgasmic bliss. I was more than okay. "Yes, I'm very okay."

Samson kissed the spot where he'd bitten me. "Mine," he blurted out.

Oh no. What the fuck did I do? I didn't belong to him. I was the daughter of an Alpha, and I was going home to claim my pack, the first Alpha female to do so. I attempted to move, but I couldn't pull away.

"Be still, Spitfire. You're not going anywhere for a while."

"Oh, yes, I am."

"We're locked together, sweetheart. Our mating triggered my knot."

Mating? Knot? I'd been so anxious to have Samson inside me that I hadn't given a thought to the consequences. I tried to remember what I knew about the wolf's knot. The lore of our culture stated that knotting happened between true mates. Lycan chemistry tied the mates together to facilitate reproduction. I could feel Samson's knot now, swollen inside me, and his mark throbbing on my neck. "Oh God. I didn't mean for this to happen."

* * *

Samson

"But your wolf did. Our wolves knew we were soulmates before we did."

"We're not soulmates, Samson."

Delilah's statement was a stab in my heart. Just a few minutes ago, she'd been so loving, so responsive. Her actions hadn't been faked or forced. She'd been on fire just as I was. I wanted more. This time I wanted to take it slow, to savor every part of her, her taste, her scent, the feel of her skin. Our wolves were right, we were made for each other. How could she think otherwise? "We're slaves to our wolf DNA. Delilah. Face it."

"If we were truly mates, why was I promised to Levi?"

"Your parents and Levi's were wrong to set up a match when you were so young. Both of you would have been unhappy. Luckily, your wolves corrected the mistake."

"It's true, Levi isn't my match, but neither are you. My destiny lies elsewhere."

"What about love? Children? If you come home with me we can have a good life together."

Delilah shook her head. "All my life, I've wanted independence and power. I would never be happy as the submissive wife of a beta."

Just then, my knot diminished and Delilah pulled away from me. I reached for her. "Stay here and talk to me."

Already she was pulling her clothes on. "We've wasted too much time. I need to get home."

A rush of possessiveness rolled through me. I didn't want to let her go. We could work this out. We just needed to talk. I could lock the door and keep her here until she came to her senses. Suddenly, I came to my senses. I'd just rescued her from one prison, and now I wanted to put her in another. She'd been through hell. She needed time to recover. "Okay, we can talk later."

I dressed hurriedly and went out to start the car. We both sat in awkward silence for the rest of the trip. I was glad when we finally reached Chicago.

Delilah's home couldn't have been more different than mine. Her pack owned an apartment building near the lake, and they all lived in it together. It was beautiful and obviously upscale, but where were the woods?

* * *

Delilah

I took Samson to my mother's apartment. She fell into my arms and started crying. I comforted her the best I could, and then introduced her to Samson. "Mother, this is Samson. He brought me home."

My mother hugged him. "Thank you for taking care of my daughter."

"I'll always take care of her." That remark went over my mother's head, but not mine, and I gave Samson a dirty look.

"The funeral is in two days," my mother said. "You must stay with us. We have a guest room."

"I'd be honored."

"Rest now, mother. I'll show Samson to his room." The guest room was large and had its own bath. I opened the drapes to let some light in. "There's a nice view of the lake."

Samson looked at me with longing. "The room is lovely, Delilah. Will you be sharing it with me?"

I stared at him, my heart pounding. He wasn't making this easy for me. "You know I can't do that. What would my mother think?"

"She'd think we were in love."

"You're crazy. This is not love, it's lust. We got it

out of our systems and now it's done."

"You know that's not true."

He crossed the room and took me in his arms. I locked my hands around his neck and pulled him toward me. Our kiss set off sparks. Our surroundings disappeared along with my resolve. The kiss grew deeper, and made me feel like nothing else mattered. I didn't want to let him go, but finally, we came up for air.

"Do you still think we've gotten it out of our systems?"

No. "Yes. The lust will end."

"You're wrong. That kiss is a beginning, not an ending. There's much more to come for us."

I shook my head. "No. This has to end." I didn't want to talk anymore. I was afraid he might convince me otherwise. "I'm starved. The kitchen must be overflowing with casseroles from the pack women. Let's check it out."

* * *

After we ate, I had pack business to attend to. Samson left to go running by the lake and I went to visit our beta, Radulf. The name suited him. It means wise wolf. Most betas are enforcers, but our beta was a sage, renowned for his wisdom. He'd been my mentor, and I'd always felt closer to him than my own father. Radulf had aged since I last saw him. His hair was silver and his face was creased with wrinkles. It made me sad.

"Hello, Uncle." He wasn't my real uncle, but that's what I called him.

The old man rose from his chair. His joints creaked as he crossed the room and grabbed me in a bear hug. "I was worried about you, Deedee. Look at my hair."

"You can't blame me for your gray hair." I laughed. He'd been going gray since he'd turned thirty. "You don't have to worry about me. I can take care of myself."

He gave me a knowing look and invited me to sit while he made coffee. We sipped from our mugs and I told him about my adventure. He seemed overtaken by emotion as he listened to my story. "I can't wait to meet your young man."

"Oh no, Uncle. He's not my young man."

Radulf stared at my neck. "Maybe he feels differently."

I brushed my hair over the bite-mark on my neck. I should have known I couldn't hide anything from him. "That was a mistake. I have more important matters to deal with."

"What could be more important than love?"

I thought for a moment. Since my father had no son, Radulf would have been in line to run the pack. I had no desire to hurt him in any way, but I had to be honest. I just hoped he wouldn't hate me. "I want a chance to show what I can do. I want to run the pack."

"I'm not surprised." He smiled. "You've always been a spitfire."

My heart jumped. It was the name Samson called me. We wolves believe in signs. Could it mean something? No. I was being silly. I took a deep breath and went on. "I don't want to take your position from you --"

He broke in. "You'll make a fine Alpha and you're not taking anything I want."

I hadn't been expecting that. "You didn't let me finish. I want to work together. Will you act as my mentor?"

"No, Deedee. I'm old and tired. I don't have

much time."

"That's not true. You have many more years."

"I'm older than your father and I'm just marking time. What good is a long life if your wife and friends are gone? All I have are my memories."

I blinked back scalding tears. "You have me."

"And I love you dearly, but I've had a full life and now I want the same for you. This is your time."

"I need you at my side."

"No, my child. Your wolf has wisely chosen the beta you need by your side. This is your destiny."

I stared at him doubtfully. "I don't know…"

"I think you do. Love is simple for a wolf. It recognizes its mate and goes after it. Things get complicated when our human side steps in. I know you're afraid you'll lose your independence, but it doesn't have to be that way. The right partner will encourage you, not hold you back." Radulf paused to let his words sink in. "When the right two become one, it's a wondrous thing. Without a partner to share the good times and the bad, your life will be lonely. Having love in your life will make you a better leader. You'll bring positive energy and enthusiasm to your pack."

Suddenly, I saw things with clarity. I sank to the floor and put my head on his knee. "I've been so stupid, Uncle. I thought I couldn't have both."

Radulf patted my head, as he had when I was a child. "It's not too late, Deedee. You have a life to live. Live it well."

"I hurt him." My voice cracked into a sob. "And he hates the city."

"Let him decide. You want to make your own choices, allow him the same opportunity."

* * *

Samson

I ran a portion of the Chicago Lakefront Trail and enjoyed it more than I wanted to admit. After a long, hot shower, I joined the ladies. We had a late dinner and I talked about my enjoyable day, but Delilah seemed determined to bring up all the negatives.

"Wasn't it crowded on such a gorgeous day?"

"Sure. There were mobs of people out, but plenty of room for everyone."

"Isn't the view beautiful?" Delilah's mother asked.

Immediately, Delilah chimed in. "You should see it in the winter when the temperature is subzero and there are piles of snow."

"I'd like to see it. I'm used to rain and snow. They're a part of life in my neck of the woods."

Delilah cleared her throat. "You must miss those woods?"

Before I could answer, Delilah's mother spoke up. "We're actually close to some great trails. They're within easy driving distance, and they give us a chance to escape the city when we feel the need."

This went on through dessert. I looked from one to the other, confused. While Delilah seemed bent on finding fault with her hometown, the older woman challenged all her comments. I wondered if it was a mother-daughter thing.

The tension ran high and I begged off early. I retired to my room, stripped and got under the covers. I grabbed a book but I couldn't concentrate. I kept thinking about the dinner conversation. If Delilah hated Chicago so much, why wouldn't she come home with me? I knew she loved me. Her wolf had made that perfectly clear. It was her human side that rejected me. Maybe she didn't want to live so close to Levi and Kya. My brain went round and round. Soon, I was fighting the heaviness in my eyelids.

* * *

I felt hands stroking me and I groaned, enjoying the dream tremendously. Fingers crept between my thighs and my swollen cock twitched every time they came close. I spread my legs under the blanket and wet heat swallowed my cock.

"Holy fuck!" *I'm not dreaming.* I opened my eyes and spotted a suspicious lump moving under the blanket as that hot mouth slid off my cock. "Don't stop."

My mysterious lover obeyed. She started to suck my balls, then returned to my cock. Heat sizzled up my spine as the suction increased. Closing my eyes, I reached under the blanket and threaded my fingers in a mane of long, thick hair. "Harder, Spitfire."

I heard a soft chuckle and the pace increased. My release came quickly.

When I opened my eyes, Delilah was sitting beside me, licking her lips. "Thank you, baby. I didn't expect that."

"What did you expect?"

"I thought I'd be spending the night alone. There was a lot of tension at dinner."

"I just wanted you to know what you were getting into."

My brow furrowed. "I don't understand."

"Did you like the way I woke you up?"

"Of course. You can wake me up like that every day."

"I intend to. When you move here."

"But I'm not --"

Delilah stopped me with a kiss, a sweet, intimate

kiss that was full of emotion. I responded eagerly and pulled her into my arms. When the kiss ended, I was more confused than ever. "What's going on, Delilah?"

"I love you, Samson."

I took her hand and pressed it over my thudding heart. "I love you, too."

"But my path is here in Chicago. I intend to take over as Alpha of my pack."

For a second I was speechless. I had had no idea that her ambitions were so high. "They won't accept you."

"I have our beta's blessing. You'll like Radulf. He's a very wise old man."

My happiness evaporated. My heart sank. "And how do I fit into this picture?"

"I thought I couldn't have both love and a vocation. He showed me that I could. I want you to be my beta."

"I want to be your husband, not someone who takes orders from you."

"I know, love. I don't intend to govern like Levi. I want you by my side, my equal, not my second in command. We'll run the pack together and protect it from the human predators."

It sounded good, and I had no family to leave behind, but I had good friends, and a community that I loved. "I need to think about it. Let's sleep on it."

Delilah looked disappointed. She made a move to leave, but I held on to her. "Stay with me. Please."

Delilah curled up in my arms and we slept.

* * *

I woke before Delilah. Not wanting to disturb her, I lay still and enjoyed the pleasure of holding her in my arms. My little Spitfire felt good lying there with me. Even better, she felt right. Cuddled in my arms and nestled against my body, she completed me, as if we were made for each other. I could have this feeling every day if I stayed. It was all I'd ever wanted, a mate and a home of my own. We belonged together. My wolf had known it all along. My human side had finally caught up.

Loving the feel of her soft curves against my hard muscles, I cuddled her close. Her scent woke my wolf and made it howl with appreciation.

* * *

Delilah

I stretched, enjoying the feeling of Samson's hard body behind me, his warm breath on my neck, his legs tangled with mine. With his arm around my waist, I felt safe and protected. I threaded my fingers with his. If only he would agree to stay here, I would be utterly content.

Samson stirred behind me. "Did I wake you?"

"Mmm… I heard your stomach rumble."

"That was my wolf. He's a randy beast."

"So I've noticed. But I'm not complaining," I hastened to add.

Samson's morning erection poked at the crease of my ass. I pushed back against it and he slid his hand up and cupped my breast, caressing it until my nipple tightened to a hard point. A shiver ran up my spine and excitement throbbed inside me.

He moved a bit to adjust his position and guided his stiff cock to my dripping pussy. I arched my back, hoping to give him a better angle, and he put a hand on my belly to brace me. Then he pushed inside. It felt so good, I moaned.

He stopped at once. "Are you okay?"

"Yes. Please don't stop."

"I never want to stop," he murmured.

I leaned back against him and he placed a hand over my pussy, moaning when he slid his middle finger between my damp folds. Heat coiled inside me, warming me inside and out.

Samson remained motionless inside me, and I writhed with frustration. "Fuck me."

"Giving orders, already, Spitfire?"

"Please fuck me."

He laughed, and started moving inside me, pulling almost all the way out, then easing back in. Each slow stroke drove me higher. I started panting.

His breath teased my neck. The friction of his facial scruff rubbing on my tender flesh was exquisite. He licked the spot where he had claimed me with his bite, letting me know what was coming. I expected his bite, but still when it came, I shattered. He sucked at the spot, driving me mad with need. A need that only he could satisfy. I'd never thought I'd respond to any man in that way. My hips jerked against him, but he held my body still and thrust inside me relentlessly. Frustrated, I whimpered while he dangled an orgasm just out of my reach.

Samson whispered in my ear, sweet words and dirty talk. I was so hot, I felt ready to climax, but I didn't want it to end. "Tell me you want me," he murmured.

"Yes, love." My voice sounded hoarse in my own ears. "I want you, Samson. Please…"

Finally, he relented. He pinched my clit and plunged deep. Pleasure made my body convulse and my legs shake. I heard him call out my name and felt his seed fill me.

We lay trembling, and caught by his knot for a very long time. When we could finally part, I didn't want to. Slick with perspiration and deliciously sated, I could have stayed that way forever.

Samson watched me with heavy-lidded eyes. "You're everything I've ever wanted, Delilah. I'm in paradise when I'm with you."

"But?"

"There are no buts. I love you."

"Forever?"

"Forever. I want to be with you, to share your dreams and raise a family."

They were the heartfelt words I wanted to hear. "Oh God, Samson, I love you so much and I was so afraid you would leave me."

"My wolf always knew I would stay. My human side took a little longer, because I felt guilty leaving the pack, but I trust my judgment and I'm following my heart."

"Will we always feel this way?"

"Yes, love. We've found our Utopia."

The Omega's Temptation (Utopia 3)
Gale Stanley

Axel, a bullied omega, has had enough of trying to please his parents and his pack. He escapes to hide among the humans, but will he reveal his true identity to save the woman he loves?

Chapter One

"This party sucks." Milo looked directly at Axel as if it was his fault. "What do you think?"

I think you're right. But Axel didn't speak out loud. Why should he? Milo didn't give a crap what an omega thought. Normally combative, the gamma wolf was obviously spoiling for a fight. It wasn't the first time Milo had bullied Axel and it wouldn't be the last.

Axel didn't take it personally. Milo didn't hate him. He didn't think Milo felt anything toward him one way or another. The gamma wolf used others to have fun with, and to make himself feel superior. It was just the nature of his wolf. Gammas were pretentious creatures, arrogant and egotistical. They viewed everyone as either strong or weak, and Axel was the weakest in the pack.

Milo leaned closer and snapped his fingers in Axel's face. "Earth to Axel."

Axel jumped. He and the other young wolves were sitting in Levi's backyard. They'd come outside to get some distance from the old heads who were partying inside the Alpha's house. The moon rose high in the sky and the twenty-somethings were looking to release some pent-up energy. Ziva, a chubby, raven-haired she-wolf Axel had once coveted, looked more than a little stoned from a joint Czar had passed to her. They were all having a good time. Except him.

Milo gave him a poke. "So, are you having a good time, Axel?"

Inwardly, Axel groaned. He'd hoped once he was outside, he'd be able to sneak away, but now Milo had put him on the spot. What could he say? He was here because of his parents. "It's where you're supposed to be," his father had warned. What twenty-one-year-old man allowed his parents to tell him what to do? Only an omega.

Axel looked up at Milo. "It's not the best party I've ever been to, but I came out of respect for the Alpha, to celebrate the birth of his first son."

Milo grinned. "Ah, yes. Pack mentality. The lowly omega is afraid to show disrespect to the Alpha."

"You're here," Axel blurted out.

Milo took a long swallow of his beer and changed the subject. "So, Axel, what was the best party you've ever been to?"

Axel sighed. "I don't remember."

Milo's grin widened. "Could it have been the Alpha's bachelor party?"

Axel's heart beat faster. He'd had enough. It was time to leave. "It's late. I'm going home." He started to rise.

Milo put a hand on Axel's shoulder and pushed him back down on the grass. The others closed in and circled him.

"The night is young. Let's play a game. Something fun like *Truth or Dare*."

Axel shook his head. "I'm tired."

"Don't be a wet blanket, Axel."

The others laughed and egged him on. Czar snorted. "He can't help it. He still wets his blanket every night."

"Fuck you."

Milo put a hand on Axel's back. "Relax. I've got your back."

"Right. Like you did at the bachelor party."

"Yes, the bachelor party. Tell us about that night. Come on, Axel. Truth or dare. Tell the true story…" Milo paused. "Or I dare you to give me a blow job."

What the fuck? "I'm straight."

Milo laughed. "So am I, but sometimes bros like to get off together."

Everyone started chanting. "Say it or suck it. Say it or suck it. Say it or suck it."

Damn Milo. And damn dear old dad for wrangling Axel an invite to the bachelor party. His parents always pushed him into uncomfortable situations, hoping he'd make friends and be accepted but it never worked out. Levi and the others were big men and they had rugged good looks. They were all into showing off their strength and sexual abilities. Axel was nothing like them, and no matter how hard he tried, he would never be one of their bromantic circle. Not that he cared; he enjoyed being on his own. Yet, he allowed himself to be pushed into these embarrassing situations time after time.

Everyone looked at him expectantly.

Trapped. Axel stood and stretched out his neck, as if straining for height amid the others. "Okay, here's the truth. I was at the bachelor party and we went to a strip club. Maybe I drank too much, but so did everyone else. It was a good time. End of story."

"That's hardly the whole story." Milo picked up where Axel left off. "It was one hell of a night. Levi was smitten with Raven and totally occupied, so we gave him some space and decided to celebrate Axel's first time at a strip club."

There were cheers and hoots. Axel felt his cheeks burn as Milo continued talking. "Axel was real shy. We bought him some drinks to loosen him up and he got shit-faced fast. I wanted him to have a good time so I bought him a few dances. We picked out a special stripper just for Axel and settled in one of the back rooms. That Alpine was one curvy woman." Milo used his hands to outline a woman with big boobs, narrow waist, and a round booty. "She was a mountain of a woman, not fat, but tall and strong like a warrior princess. For a nice tip, she'd do whatever you wanted. I'll never forget the look on Axel's face when Alpine walked into that room. He took one look and froze."

Milo started laughing. "Damn, he looked like a deer in the headlights, paralyzed with fear. Then the music started up and Alpine shimmied closer to Axel. She started grinding on him. He was so stiff he looked like he was afraid to move. Alpine told him to relax and she started clambering all over him like a dog, licking his face with a big wet tongue. It was cringe worthy. When the music stopped, Axel tried to get up, but Alpine pushed him back down in the chair. I'd paid in advance for three dances and Alpine intended to deliver." Milo paused for effect.

Czar shouted out, "What happened next?"

"Axel stuck with it like a trooper, until Alpine started to get creative. By that time, she was completely naked and shoving her ass in his face. Suddenly Axel started heaving. He threw up everywhere, and I mean everywhere. Alpine's ass was covered in puke. Boy, was she pissed. She stormed out of the room, and I followed, shoving money into her hands. When I got back, Axel was bawling like a baby and trying to clean himself up. Samson and I took him to the bathroom and cleaned him up as best we could."

Czar yelled, "What a dork." Everyone laughed and Milo laughed the hardest. He slapped Axel on the back. "It was spectacular. I'll never forget it."

Neither will I.

Ziva shouted, "Let's keep playing. Milo told Axel's story, so Axel needs another turn. Truth or dare, Axel? Have you ever fucked?"

Could this night get any worse? Sex was a sensitive subject for Axel. He liked to think he was saving himself for his soulmate, but truth be told, he found it hard to get a date. And everyone knew it.

Axel had enough. He would not talk about his sex life and he would not give these idiots the satisfaction of embarrassing him any further. He swallowed his anger and mumbled, "I don't kiss and tell."

Milo smirked. "Stop stalling. This is *Truth or Dare*. You have to tell."

Axel's eyes narrowed as Milo taunted him. The fire inside him burned hotter. Axel's knuckles turned white from clenching his fists.

Still, Milo wouldn't let it go. "Have you ever fucked? Yes or no?"

Axel snapped. His rage boiled over and he lunged at Milo. Milo merely smiled and stepped aside, and Axel flew past him, landing flat on his face. Behind him, Axel heard loud, raucous laughter. He had to get away from that sound. Axel regained his balance, rose to his feet, and started running. He didn't slow down until he neared his house.

The pack lived in a small, remote town in upstate New York. Everybody knew everybody. It should have been idyllic, a place where everyone actually cared for one another. Instead, it was a place where everyone mocked him. Axel didn't want to live that way anyway more. No one deserved to be constantly humiliated.

It was time to surround himself with kind people, or at least strangers who didn't know him and wouldn't pick on him. It was time to leave the pack.

* * *

The baby stirred and let out a howl, rescuing Cassie from her all too frequent nightmare. She'd left home six months ago, but she still couldn't forget the horror that had driven her away.

Benjamin Carlton.

They'd met in college. Cassie was a freshman, a naïve, small-town girl hoping to be a veterinarian someday. She'd grown up in Punxsutawney, PA, best known for being the home of a groundhog. A college scholarship took her to the University of Arizona, where she met Benjamin at a frat party. He was a senior, studying for a business degree, and extremely good-looking, tall and muscular with black hair and dark, intense eyes. All the girls fancied him, but he only had eyes for Cassie. They flirted all night and then he walked her back to her dorm and asked for her phone number.

The next day he texted Cassie five times. Thrilled, but wary, she wondered why he wanted her of all the girls he could have. A red flag went up, but she agreed to have dinner with him.

Conversation came easy. They talked about their goals and traded stories about the past. Their childhoods were very different. Cassie had helicopter parents, so overprotective that they practically disowned her when she left home. Benjamin came from a wealthy New York family and he'd been raised by nannies. He confessed to a lonely childhood. "To this day, I still feel alone in a crowd of people," he'd said. "I have trouble connecting."

Cassie sympathized. She wanted Benjamin to feel connected to her, and that night she lost her virginity to him.

Before long, Cassie was seeing Benjamin every day. Her friends offered up dire warnings, telling her that Benjamin was rushing the relationship forward too quickly. Cassie didn't want to hear it and eventually her friends drifted away.

Benjamin was intense and he came on strong, but Cassie thrived on his attention, thrilled that such an intelligent, handsome man wanted her.

The end of the school year was fast approaching. Benjamin would be graduating and moving back home. He never talked about their future and Cassie feared that it would be the end of them. She tried to tell Benjamin that their relationship could survive the long distance, but he always changed the subject. Cassie thought she knew how he felt. They'd be over 2,000 miles apart and she didn't like to think about it, either.

The weeks flew by, and graduation was looming when Cassie realized her period was late. She wasn't too concerned, Benjamin always used condoms, but she bought a pregnancy test to be sure. When the two blue lines appeared, Cassie stared at them, not believing she had seen right. She took another test. It was still positive. Cassie peered at her shocked reflection in the bathroom mirror. *I'm not ready.*

Once the feelings of surprise, denial, and terror wore off, Cassie was happy and excited about the new life growing inside her. Benjamin would be, too. She was sure of it. This was life changing but Benjamin would take it in stride. He was her everything. She'd mapped her life around him -- graduation, marriage, work, pregnancy. They were just doing things out of order. But they loved each other. Somehow, they would make it work.

A few days later, Benjamin took her to a nice restaurant. Cassie assumed he wanted to talk about their future and she felt ready to reveal her big news.

She protested as Benjamin ordered a bottle of wine. He ordered it anyway and filled their glasses. He took a big sip and set his glass down. "Graduation is around the corner and I'll be leaving for New York. We need to talk, Cassie."

"I know." Cassie's heart beat a little faster. "I have something --"

"We're at different stages in our lives," Benjamin talked over her. "And a long-distance relationship won't work. I'll be taking a spot in the family business and I won't have time to travel back and forth."

Hurt, Cassie blurted out. "That's what I wanted to tell you. You won't have to travel. I decided to put off school for a while. I'll just move with you and --"

"It's out of the question."

Tears slid down her cheeks. "Why? What did I do wrong? Tell me and I'll fix it."

"It's not you, it's me. I need time to establish myself. I can't worry about starting my career and taking care of you."

He's dumping me. Cassie's hurt morphed into anger. "It's a little late to worry about that. I'm pregnant."

Benjamin's expression grew hard and resentful. "How could you let this happen?"

"Me? You always took care of the protection."

"I assumed you were on the pill. I used condoms to prevent STDs. Is it too late to… you know? Take care of things? I'll pay for everything. You'll be able to finish school."

"I'll take care of things my own way. I intend to have this baby." Heartbroken, Cassie pushed her chair back and fled the restaurant.

Benjamin called the next day and apologized profusely. "You just took me by surprise. Of course you'll have the baby. We'll leave for New York together."

Cassie felt uncertain about his true feelings, but

she shrugged off her doubts and agreed to move with him. After all, the baby came first. She'd never be able to support the child on her own, and Benjamin had a good career waiting for him. The baby would bring them together again and they would have the future she'd imagined.

Benjamin picked out an expensive apartment in New York. Cassie kept busy decorating the second bedroom as a nursery while Benjamin spent most of his time at the office. The loving relationship she hoped for never happened. No longer did Benjamin treasure her company or take her to bed with unbridled passion. He worked night and day, and he drank too much. Often, he came home in a rage that he took out on Cassie. When she cried, he would yell at her, "Stop bawling. You got what you wanted."

They argued constantly and the distance between them grew. After one particularly bad fight, Benjamin shoved her against the wall and struck her in the face. Cassie feared him, but she felt powerless to fight back.

If only she had someone to talk to, but it was hard to make friends in New York and Cassie rarely saw his family. When she did, they were cold and unwelcoming.

Cassie felt heavy in body and mind, lost and alone, but she blamed herself for their problems. After all, she'd burdened him with the added stress of a family on top of the pressure of a new career. Because of her guilt, she endured the misery he put her through.

Cassie's contractions started one night when Benjamin was working late. She called his office and his cell phone and left messages on both. He never returned her calls. Her contractions became stronger and her water broke. Cassie had no choice but to call a cab and go to the hospital alone. The baby was born two hours later.

Benjamin arrived at the hospital the next morning, with a large bouquet and a story about a deal he was trying to close. He made a huge fuss over his son, calling him his mini-me. Once again, Cassie put her doubts aside and forgave him.

Now that the baby was here, Cassie suggested that it was time to tie the knot. Despite insisting they name the baby, Benjamin Carlton, Junior, Benjamin said they should wait until Cassie got her figure back before they married. Hurt and disappointed, Cassie dropped the subject of marriage.

She threw herself into caring for Benny. He had colic and she spent many sleepless nights walking around the apartment trying to soothe him. One day he had an especially bad bout and Cassie spent the whole day trying to calm him down. When Benjamin came home, she was in the rocker cuddling the baby, who'd finally quieted down.

Benjamin looked at her with contempt. "Don't you have anything better to do?"

Shocked, Cassie stared back at him. "What could be better than caring for our baby?"

"Get a job. Contribute. Or at least have dinner ready when I get home." He stormed out and Cassie didn't see him the rest of the night.

Things only got worse after that. Nothing Cassie did was right. She didn't press Ben's shirts the way he liked them. The meals she prepared were tasteless. If he'd had a bad day at work, he took it out on her. His insults grew in intensity. She was stupid and lazy. He ridiculed her. Cassie felt like less than nothing, but after his rants, she always accepted his apologies, meek as a kitten. He loved the baby and spared no expense for Junior's needs, so Cassie placated him as best she could and life went on.

Until it didn't.

Junior turned two, a good-natured, active baby, but he had some terrible-two moments. Cassie took them in stride, but Benjamin did not. He blamed Cassie, accused her of coddling the boy. And he yelled. A lot.

Cassie tried to have Benny fed and asleep before Benjamin came home, but one night he walked in during Junior's feeding. The baby didn't want his carrots and Cassie was ready to give up.

"You're home all day and you can't even feed the boy. Get up. I'll see that he gets his vegetables."

Benjamin tried a few times with no luck. Finally, he shoved the spoon in Benny's mouth. The two-year-old spit out the mouthful, picked up his bowl, and threw it at Benjamin's $4,000 Tom Ford suit. Benjamin's temper went from 0 to 100 in an instant and he slapped the baby. Hard.

An angry red handprint formed on Benny's chubby cheek and he screamed louder than ever before.

Bile rose in Cassie's throat. In that moment, what remained of their relationship shattered to pieces. "You monster!" Curses exploded from Cassie's mouth. From the look in Benjamin's eyes, she knew immediately that they'd hit their mark.

His eyes went wide with shock. It was the first time she'd defied him. "You ungrateful little bitch," he shouted. "Your brat is just like you."

His eyes popped as they traded insults. He got in Cassie's face, and foaming like a rabid dog, he spat obscenities at her. Cassie wiped his spit from her cheek and backed away, but he followed. There was no time to duck and cover. Exploding with unrestrained fury, he slugged her. Cassie's scream set the baby off again.

"This is bedlam. I've had enough." Benjamin stormed off and Cassie heard the door slam behind him.

Cassie picked up her son and tried to comfort him. Benny was crying so hard he couldn't catch his breath. He clung to Cassie and she sobbed along with him. It took forever until they both calmed down. Benjamin had hit her a few times in the past, but he'd never hit the baby before. This changed everything. She could never trust him around her child. The sleeping tiger inside her awoke. It was time to pack her fucking bags and leave.

Cassie had no idea where she was going. She only knew she had to put distance between her and Benny, and Benjamin. She had enough money to fill the tank of the second-hand Toyota Benjamin had finally purchased so she could take Junior to his doctor appointments. With the baby sound asleep in the car seat, she started driving.

Cassie was afraid Benjamin would follow them and panic racked her the whole time. She needn't have worried. Benjamin had probably stayed out all night and didn't even know they'd left.

They made a few stops for gas and food. It wasn't until they reached Philadelphia that Cassie decided to stick around. She knew immediately that it would be a good place for her and Benny to stay, at least for a few days. A few days turned into months. Cassie found peace in Philadelphia, something she'd lacked for longer than she cared to admit. The city was big enough to blend in, but it was composed of neighborhoods that felt, well, neighborly. She hoped that here she could forget the past, but it wasn't that simple. Benjamin was unpredictable. He could show up any time. Cassie had to remain vigilant. She was careful to never reveal too much of her life or get too close to anyone.

Cassie pushed aside thoughts of the past. She needed to feed the baby and get them both dressed. After breakfast, she packed a diaper bag with his things and prepared to drop him off at daycare before heading to her job at the diner. She didn't like leaving him, but it couldn't be helped; she had to work.

Cassie tossed a glance over her shoulder to make sure no one was following them. It might be silly to think Benjamin would be lurking nearby; he was probably glad to be rid of them, but she took no chances. The thought of seeing him again made her shiver. He was such a mean-spirited, vengeful person, and she knew how he loved to get the last word. If he ever found them... No. She had to focus on their new life. Hopefully there were no clues to link them to Philadelphia. They lived a quiet life, and had few friends. Cassie had learned her lesson.

Chapter Two

Axel wanted a different life for himself, but he felt conflicted. Change might be easy for some, but not for him. He'd never been far from home, and the thought of leaving everyone and everything he knew sent chills down his spine. Already, he doubted his motives.

He tried to think of this as an adventure, a series of amazing possibilities awaiting him, but it didn't help. His idea of adventure had always meant shifting and going for a run in the woods. This could be a risky endeavor. But what choice did he have?

The more I try to please others, the more I ignore my own wants and needs. The longer I stay with the pack, the more the fear of what others think of me holds me back. That's not acceptable.

Just do it, he told himself. *Leave before you change your mind.* A more perfect opportunity might never come. His parents were still at the party and would probably be there for several more hours. If he left now, he could avoid an ugly argument.

Axel packed a bag and left a cryptic note for his parents. Just a few lines informing them he would write soon. He didn't want them to know where he was going. Hell. He didn't even know where he was going. Axel wanted to settle in a place where nobody knew him, a place where no one would have unrealistic expectations of him. Was there such a place?

Axel didn't own a car and bus tickets were expensive. Hitchhiking would have to be his mode of transportation. He started walking along the deserted back road that led to the highway. The familiar woods beckoned to him and the trees whispered. *Don't go. Stay with us.*

He could do that easily. Morph, and lose himself in the forest. No. A feral life wasn't for him. It would mean living in a black and white world, no books, no conversation, no human contact. Living as a beast was a last resort. He forced himself to put one foot in front of the other and keep walking.

Finally, the road merged with the highway, and Axel breathed a sigh of relief that he'd made it this far. In this sparsely populated area, at this late hour, it would be tough to get a ride, even tougher because people were afraid to pick up strangers these days. Humans were now aware that there were shifters living among them and they couldn't tell the difference between another human or a shifter. That made them fearful. Axel didn't blame them. Not all shifters were good, and only the bad ones ended up on TV or the Internet.

Shifters were being blamed for every crime, and there were dire warnings about mutants and freaks using their animal abilities to take over the country. The media exaggerated every incident because it made good copy. They fed humanity's fears by stressing shifter strength and cunning.

Most shifters just ignored the prejudice and formed their own communities. Living with the pack hadn't been satisfying, but it had been safe. Living among the humans might be dangerous. What if someone found out he was a shifter? They might drive him out of town or even kill him. He'd have to be very cautious and hide his real identity. If only he could live his entire life with the pack, but there was no place for him among his own kind. He might as well take his chances with the humans.

Anxiety crept up Axel's spine. What a joke. People called him a beast, but suddenly he felt like prey. What if a serial killer stopped and offered him a ride? Maybe a bus would have been safer, but thumbing a ride was cheaper, and he needed to save what little money he had. He hadn't been working regularly.

Axel tried to shake off the road willies. *Man up. You can fit in.* He looked like a harmless human. At a lean five foot ten, one hundred and fifty pounds, he looked younger than his twenty-one years. He sighed and pulled his baseball cap down over his eyes.

An engine sounded, and Axel saw lights in the distance. He stuck out his thumb.

* * *

Many rides later, Axel had lost count, the driver stopped and turned to him. "Sorry, buddy. This is the end of the road."

"Where are we?"

"Philadelphia, the City of Brotherly Love."

City of Brotherly Love. Sounds like a good omen.

Axel thanked the driver and got out of the car. He needed sleep and a place to stow his suitcase before he explored the city. Luckily, there was a motel nearby. He paid for a room, and exhausted, fell into a dreamless sleep.

* * *

Axel woke to sunlight streaming through the blinds. After a shower and a quick breakfast at a coffee shop, he started exploring. Luckily, Philadelphia was a city easily traversed by foot or bus. Axel found himself in a city of vibrant neighborhoods, each one with its own distinctive personality. How could he identify the right community for a lone wolf?

Wherever he went, Axel checked rentals, but he couldn't seem to find the perfect spot. Late in the afternoon, gray clouds drifted in and Axel felt raindrops on his face. He spotted a café and ducked inside to avoid the rain. The small restaurant was warm and cheery, and filled with intriguing aromas. He realized he was famished and he found an empty table by the window. Axel slid into a chair and watched people rush by as they tried to outrun the raindrops.

"What can I get you?"

Axel turned to the waitress and his gaze locked with hers. Suddenly and without warning, his heart began to race. Thank God, he was sitting because his legs went weak and an incessant throbbing started between them. He pulled at his collar. His clothes felt way too tight. A shudder of excitement mixed with apprehension shook his body.

The waitress looked tired, but there was a spark of kindness in her bright blue gaze. Maybe even a spark of something else. Axel studied her for a moment. No, it must be his imagination. His loneliness made him see things that weren't there. Undoubtedly, that pleasant expression greeted all her diners. He wished that it were for him alone.

This was so unlike him. When the others in his pack saw an attractive woman, they immediately thought about sex. But not Axel. He was waiting for his soulmate and he knew his wolf would guide him in her direction.

Being drawn to the waitress was surely an aberration. Consorting with a human was forbidden. She tempted him, but it could never be. Still, he could fantasize. Couldn't he?

Axel looked at the name embroidered on her uniform. *Cassie*. A pretty name for a pretty girl. Tiny, she appeared shorter than Axel, a small, frail human. Axel's protective instincts kicked in. He tamped down his compassion, and his arousal, reminding himself again that Cassie was human. Had he already forgotten his vow to be guarded? Showing his infatuation would only get him into trouble.

"Would you like to order now?"

Suddenly fully present, Axel looked up and offered back a friendly smile. Cassie would know the menu better than anyone, what was good and what was not so good. At least she could recommend a good meal. "I've never been here before, Cassie. What do you recommend?"

"The special today is pot roast. It's very good."

"Perfect. I'll have that. And water, please."

"Coming right up."

Axel was glad he'd trusted her judgment because the pot roast was excellent. He dug in with gusto. When he glanced up, he caught Cassie looking his way. Their gazes locked and Axel felt a jolt, as if a doctor had put paddles on his chest and given him an electric shock. This time he knew Cassie felt it too. She blushed and turned away quickly. A jerk in his pants convinced him he wasn't imagining their mutual interest.

All through the rest of his meal, Axel questioned his feelings. This mysterious attraction was shocking. Everyone knew that like attracted like. Birds of a feather, and all that stuff. This connection, whether real or not, worried him. He hadn't left home for romance. His priority was a place to live. Perhaps he should cross East Falls off his list.

When at last he pushed his empty plate aside, Cassie returned with the bill. She didn't look him in the eye as she placed it before him. Axel didn't want to seem like a speechless idiot, but he couldn't think of a thing to say. Finally, he asked if she knew where he could find an inexpensive room to rent. Flustered, Cassie reeled off a few addresses.

Axel thanked her, and left a good tip, but not too good. He didn't want to come off as a creep.

It was getting late, but he was already here, so he checked out Cassie's recommendations. None of her suggestions suited him and he took it as a sign to move on. As he started looking for the bus stop, Axel came upon a lovely brownstone with a vacancy sign in the window. He rang the bell and an older woman came to the door. She introduced herself as Mrs. May, and showed him efficiency, a one-room apartment with bath. It had a kitchenette built into one of the walls and an alcove for sleeping. It was enough for Axel and the price was right. He gave his new landlady a deposit.

This might be a mistake, but Axel felt lucky that he'd stumbled onto a cheap apartment in a decent area. So far, Philadelphia seemed reasonably affordable and not all that impossible to navigate. The many parks guaranteed he'd still get his fill of green space. Before he could stop himself, another thought crossed his mind.

And there's a great café in walking distance.

* * *

Axel's talent for repairing cars had led him to a career as a car mechanic. He found it rewarding to make broken down vehicles run again. Unfortunately for him, shifters didn't drive much, so he'd never made a lot of money. It was one of the reasons he'd still lived at home with his parents. He hoped things would be different here, because his savings wouldn't last much longer. Luckily, it took only two days to find a job at a local garage -- J and P Auto Service. Pete, an older man with gray hair and a matching beard, joked that he would hire Axel because he liked his name. In reality,

Pete had recently lost his long-time partner, Jack, and he needed help badly. Axel appreciated the chance, and promised to do a good job.

The next morning, Axel rose early, and at 5:45 he opened his apartment door to leave for work. To his surprise, a young boy toddled out the door of the adjoining apartment and waved to him.

"Hi, buddy."

"Hi." The smiling youngster approached and put up a hand for a high five.

Axel grinned and reciprocated.

"Benny, where are --" Cassie came running out of the apartment and grabbed the boy. For a moment, she and Axel just stood and stared at each other. Then Cassie frowned. "Are you following us?"

She's married. Overwhelmed with disappointment, Axel managed to blurt out. "No. Of course not."

Cassie didn't look convinced, but she apologized. "I'm sorry. I don't like him to talk to strangers."

"I'm not a stranger." Axel held out his hand. "But we were never formally introduced. My name is Axel Randulf."

Cassie held onto her boy and ignored his outstretched hand. "Cassie Miller."

Axel looked at the boy. "And what's your name?"

"Benny Carlton."

"Benny Carlton Miller?"

The youngster shook his head. "No. Benny Carlton."

"I'm not married," Cassie said sharply. "And I'm going to be late for work."

Axel's spirits soared. He tried to hide his smile. "Oh, sorry. Me, too. Not married, and late for work. I'll see --"

Before he could finish his sentence, Cassie slammed her door shut. Carrying Benny, she pushed past him and ran down the steps.

Confused, Axel looked after them. What had he done to piss her off? And why hadn't Cassie told him about the vacancy here? Obviously, she'd wanted to keep him at a distance.

Somehow he'd found the apartment anyway. Like others of his kind, Axel believed in signs and omens. Maybe his wolf was directing his path. There had to be a reason he'd ended up next door to Cassie, even though she wasn't happy to see him. For now, Axel chalked up Cassie's behavior to being an overprotective parent. That he could understand. But he would stay away from the coffee shop for a while. No need to create an awkward situation there.

Axel's morning hadn't started out great, but his first day at the garage went well. Pete seemed surprised at how quickly Axel could diagnose a car that had broken down. Axel worked late and grabbed a sandwich with Pete. When he got home, he was too tired to think about anything.

The next day, he left for work a little earlier to avoid Cassie, but evidently she had had the same idea. Once again, they ran into each other in the hall. Axel waved to the boy and offered up a nervous smile. "We have to stop meeting like this."

Cassie grumbled something and made a hasty exit.

Well, if that's the way you want it... Pissed, Axel waited a moment, and then left. He didn't have time for this bullshit.

Axel put in a busy week at J and P, and Pete complimented his work. Near closing time on Friday,

Axel went in the back, and started to remove his coveralls. He heard Pete calling him, so he buttoned up again and went out front. To his surprise, he saw Cassie standing next to a battered Toyota. Silently, they glared at each other.

Pete looked confused. "You two know each other?"

"Hardly," Cassie said.

"I ate in the café once," Axel explained.

"And he lives in my building," Cassie added.

"Well," Pete said. "It's a small world. Axel, meet Cassie. Cassie, meet Axel. Axel is a bang-up mechanic and he'll take good care of your baby. The Toyota, I mean."

"Right," Cassie said, as she got her son out of the car seat. The boy waved to Pete and Axel.

"I'll get right to it." Axel wanted to make a good impression. "I'll stay late tonight and work on it."

"That's not necessary," Cassie said. "Tomorrow will be fine. Just let me know what it'll cost. Goodnight, Pete." She turned and walked out.

Pete scrutinized Axel. "She's normally a sweet gal, works hard and takes care of her son. Don't know what's gotten into her. Did you two have some kind of falling out?"

Axel shook his head. "I don't know why she doesn't like me." *But I'm going to find out.*

* * *

Frustrated, Cassie walked home deep in thought. *Why do I keep running into this man?* It couldn't just be coincidence. Could he be working for Benjamin? Why had she agreed to have him work on her car? What if he put a tracking device on it? Why hadn't she changed her name? Damn it. She'd left Benjamin in such a hurry, and she'd needed ID and her Social

Security number to get a job.

Her life had been going so well. She'd thought they were safe. Now she worried that she might have to pick up everything and leave. It just wasn't fair.

* * *

After Axel replaced Cassie's distributor cap and rotor, he thought things would improve between them, but Cassie remained distant. Disappointed, Axel concentrated on work and exploring his new neighborhood. He had to admit that his new life was moving along smoothly. Pete appreciated his work in the garage and even promised him a raise in six months if it continued. Except for the friction between him and Cassie, it was a life without stress and humiliation.

Axel enjoyed the daily structure -- waking up early, going to work, fixing himself a meal. No tormentors harassed him. No one had unrealistic expectations of him. For the first time he had his own space, and he treasured his tiny apartment and his solitude. No one back home had valued him because he was different. As part of the pack, he'd struggled. Now he realized that making a new life for himself had been the right decision.

But there were drawbacks. The weekends were full of empty time he tried to fill with running in the park. Those were the times that thoughts of Cassie came back to haunt him. Her blue eyes and honey-colored hair seemed permanently etched in his brain. Sometimes he imagined he could smell her scent. He pushed aside those memories. Obviously, she didn't feel the same. Cassie had seemed pleased with the work he'd done on her car, but she hadn't become any friendlier. In fact, she had to be avoiding him, because they didn't run into each other anymore. Until the day they did.

* * *

Late for work, Axel shot out the front door and took the steps two at a time. He was surprised to see Cassie just a few feet ahead of him, gripping Benny's hand. The boy's other hand clutched a brightly colored ball. The ball dropped and rolled across the street. Benny pulled away from his mother and took off after it.

From the corner of his eye, Axel saw a car heading straight for Benny. Without stopping to think, he darted into the street and pushed the boy out of the way. Axel's body flew up and hit the hood of the car. He bounced and went flying again. When he landed on the cement, he felt bones break and muscles bruise. Then everything went black.

Chapter Three

Consciousness pulled at Axel, but he resisted and reached out for the darkness.

The next time he opened his eyes he saw a beautiful blonde angel looking down at him with a worried expression.

"Cassie?" he whispered.

"Axel. You're awake."

"Where am I?" he mumbled.

"The hospital. You've been in a coma since they brought you in yesterday."

Suddenly, his memory came back in a rush. "Benny?"

"He's fine. Thanks to you. He's here in the children's ward for precautionary reasons. You saved his life, Axel. I don't know how to thank you."

"Knowing he's okay is enough for me."

Cassie's eyes filled with tears. "When I think of how miserably I've treated you…"

"It's okay. I know what it's like to be wary of strangers."

"I'm not wary anymore. Can we be friends?"

Suddenly, Axel felt a whole lot better. "I'd like that."

Cassie reached for his hand. "How are you? Are you in pain? The doctors say there may be internal injuries. They're going to run more tests."

"Don't worry about me. I'll be fine." Axel started pulling at the gauze around his torso. He looked down. The bruises on his flesh had already faded. "In fact, I'm better already."

Cassie's blue eyes went wide. "How is that possible?"

Shit. How do I explain my ability to heal so quickly?

Like the others of his kind, Axel was able to heal himself in a way humans could only imagine. He hadn't been in a coma. He'd gone into a deep, dark sleep that allowed his body to regenerate. But he could never tell that to Cassie. Axel blurted out a half-truth. "Genetics. Everyone in my family heals quickly."

Cassie's brow furrowed with confusion and Axel quickly changed the subject. "I need to see Benny." He sat up and threw his legs over the side of the bed. "And then go to work."

Cassie tried to push him back down. "No work today. I called Pete. He said to take as much time as you need."

Axel waved his arm around the room. "I can't take off. How will I pay for all this?"

Cassie smiled. "You're a hero. Pete said that you're not to worry about the hospital bills. He'll take care of everything that the donations don't cover."

"Donations?" Axel stood and pulled the hospital gown around his body. "I don't like charity. I'll pay him back. Every penny." He looked around the room for his clothes. "I want to see Benny now."

Cassie sighed. "I guess there's no stopping you." She went to the closet and retrieved his clothes. "I'll wait for you outside."

Ten minutes later, they entered Benny's room in the children's ward. Excited to see his mother and Axel's familiar face, he started waving.

Axel grabbed him in a big bear hug just as a doctor walked in to speak to Cassie. "Your son is fine. I'm going to discharge him." The doctor took a closer look at Axel. "Weren't you admitted with the boy?"

"Yes, but I'm fine now. I'm leaving with him."

Suddenly Axel found himself surrounded by white coats, doctors intent on keeping him in the hospital while Axel insisted he only needed to rest and recuperate at home. The arguments went on and on. Benny started crying. Finally, someone gave Axel a medical liability waiver to sign, and they let him leave. He breathed a sigh of relief and hoped they'd forget all about him.

After that, the friction between Axel and Cassie disappeared. They didn't become lovers, not by a long shot, but Axel started eating at the café and Cassie always had a smile and a wave for him. She looked genuinely happy to have him in her section. He tried not to make too much of it, knowing she felt beholden to him for saving Benny. He kept a little distance and he didn't tip crazy high. He didn't want her to get the wrong idea.

What was the right idea? Deep down, Axel knew if Cassie gave him any encouragement, he'd jump at the chance to fuck her. Cassie was his first real crush. She treated him with respect and admired his work ethic. Every day they became better friends. He'd like more, a real relationship, but there were too many obstacles between them, the main one being they were two different species. He could never reveal his origins. Cassie would fear him and she wouldn't let him near Benny. That would kill Axel for sure; he'd become very fond of the boy.

Axel suspected that Cassie kept her own secrets. She presented herself as confident and self-assured, but hidden below the surface, Axel sensed a vulnerability born of fear. Someone had hurt her in the past and it had to be Benny's father. She never talked about him and Axel didn't pry. How could he when he wouldn't shed his own mask?

* * *

Cassie enjoyed Axel's company, and he was

great with Benny. It was nice to have a male figure for Benny to look up to, but Cassie feared the growing physical attraction between her and Axel. It went way beyond friendship. It was emotional and romantic and physical, all in one. She didn't think she'd ever again feel that way for a man, and yet, every time she saw Axel she had a strong desire to touch and be touched. One day she feared she'd give in to those feelings.

No, I'm not ready. I have to heal before I let another man into my life. That's years in the future. Besides, Axel doesn't need a traumatized woman with a child and all kinds of baggage.

She could make all the excuses she wanted but Axel was already in her life. If only she could tell if her feelings were real and lasting. She'd been fooled before, putting her trust in a man who'd abused her and Benny.

Axel was nothing like Benjamin. They were as opposite as two men could be. Except... Axel had secrets. In the hospital, Axel had mentioned his good genes and his family, but he'd never spoken of them again. When Cassie asked him about his past, he always changed the subject.

Can I really hold that against him? Who am I to judge someone for having secrets when I'm hiding behind a mask, afraid that the world is going to find me out?

* * *

One Friday morning, Axel and Cassie were having coffee in her apartment before leaving for work. This had become a regular routine, one that Cassie enjoyed very much. Benny had finished breakfast and he sat on the floor pouring over a book. He pointed at the pages. "Wabbit, wabbit, wabbit."

"Yes, peanut, it's a rabbit." Cassie turned to Axel. "He loves animals. I think it's time for a visit to the zoo."

"That's a great idea. I've never been to a zoo."

Cassie felt her face heat. "Oh, I didn't mean to put you on the spot."

"Nonsense. I want to go and it'll be more fun with you and Benny."

"Well, okay. How about tomorrow? We're both off."

"It's a date."

Oh my God. A date? Don't spaz out, Cassie. It's not a real date, just an outing with Benny. "Yes. Now, we better get moving. I still have to drop Benny at day care and we'll be late for work."

All day, Cassie thought about *the date,* excited and fearful at the same time. That night, she found it hard to fall asleep.

When Saturday morning finally arrived, she was a nervous wreck. She might have canceled, except Benny would have been so disappointed.

A knock at the door made her heart speed up. As soon as she let Axel in, Benny leaped at him. "Go, go, go."

Cassie laughed. "Just give me a minute, peanut. Have a seat, Axel. I need to pack a few things."

Axel eyed the huge bag she was filling. "A few things?"

A list of items rolled off Cassie's tongue. "Water, sunscreen, bandages, wipes, hand sanitizer, change of clothes, camera…" Cassie stopped to think. "I packed a lunch, and the stroller is in the car. I think that's it."

Axel looked amazed. "I never realized it took so much to travel with a toddler."

Cassie looked at Axel carefully. He was childless and younger than her, and she wondered if he would really enjoy spending so much time with Benny. Well, she'd know by the end of the day.

Axel hefted Benny and Cassie toted the bag. She helped Axel buckle Benny into the car seat and off they went. It didn't take more than fifteen minutes to reach the zoo, and there was ample parking at the adjacent parking garage.

"Let's go, go, go," Axel said.

Benny echoed him. The boys sounded so enthusiastic, the excitement rubbed off on Cassie. Just north of the entrance, they stopped at the Meerkat Maze.

"Wabbits!" Benny shrieked as he watched the rambunctious mammals. Cassie and Axel laughed, enjoying his excitement.

Benny loved the big cats, too, but the coolest attraction was twenty feet up, an animal travel system where they saw monkeys walking overhead. Then a stop at the KidZooU, an indoor and outdoor exhibit with a small playground, and a petting farm where Benny brushed the goats.

After Cassie's delicious lunch, Benny started yawning, and Cassie knew he wouldn't last much longer, but no zoo outing was complete without a ride on the Amazon Rainforest Carousel. Axel sat Benny atop one of the reptile seats and Cassie took lots of photos. They even squeezed in a Pony Ride before Benny became cranky and started screaming for Cassie's attention.

"I'm sorry, Axel. I think he's overtired."

Axel crouched down and made eye contact with Benny. "I'm tired, too, little man." He offered the boy a drink. "Whatta ya say we head home and rest. Later, I'll show you how to draw the animals we saw."

Benny's tears dried up and he held out his arms so Axel could lift him.

Cassie was amazed. "How did you avoid a total meltdown?"

Axel grinned. "We're buddies. We understand each other."

Cassie breathed a sigh of relief. She had her answer. Axel was not faking it. He was genuinely fond of Benny and adept at handling her son's moods.

Benny slept on the way home. Axel carried him in, and Cassie, unwilling to let the day end, invited him to stay for a while.

* * *

Grateful for the invitation, Axel stayed. He stood by the bedroom door and watched Cassie settle Benny in the crib. He wondered how the boy's father could stay away from such a sweet, lovable child. He must be dead.

Axel had already become so attached to the boy, he couldn't imagine not having Benny in his life. Axel was young, but anxious to have his own family. Shifters, men as well as women, had biological clocks ticking away. When they met their soulmate, baby fever really kicked in, compelling them to create families. It was a biological imperative to increase their species. Cassie was different, but that didn't keep Axel from wanting her. He'd love to give Benny a brother or sister. His pack didn't have to know. But it wasn't fair to Cassie. How could he give her a half-breed child and condemn her to a life of hiding?

Cassie turned and held a finger to her lips, putting an end to his thoughts. Feeling confused, Axel walked away and sat in the living room. Cassie left the bedroom door ajar so she could hear Benny if he woke. Then she joined Axel on the couch. They both spoke at once.

"Today was wonderful."

Axel grinned. "You first."

"Thank you for today." Cassie leaned forward and her mouth brushed his.

Axel was completely unprepared. He'd stared at Cassie's lips so often, but he'd never imagined how soft and warm they would feel against his own. Instinctively, he opened his mouth, their breaths mingled, and Cassie let out a gentle moan.

On the few dates Axel had experienced back home, he'd always felt awkward, but there was no awkwardness now. He and Cassie came together as if they'd been made for each other.

Their kiss turned passionate and Axel's breathing quickened. His senses were seduced and he couldn't think straight. Drunk on endorphins, he wanted more.

Instinctively, Axel put his shaky hands on Cassie's hips and pulled her closer. She drew in a sharp breath and looked into his eyes.

Axel stared back, mesmerized. *Stop*, he told himself. Instead, he found himself saying. "I don't want this to end. That kiss was a good beginning, but there's so much more to experience."

Still, he wasn't ready to penetrate her. Intercourse would take their relationship to a new level. It would make them a couple and Axel had so many unanswered questions holding him back. Could he hurt her, emotionally or physically? He'd never forgive himself.

* * *

When Axel finally pulled back, he left Cassie breathless. She'd initiated the kiss, but she'd never thought it would be so intimate, so electrifying. Axel felt it, too. He looked into her eyes while he smoothed his hands over her back, her arms, wherever he could reach. His gentle caresses felt so good, Cassie didn't want him to stop. It had been a long time since a man had touched her like this. Her panties grew damp as arousal pulsed between her thighs. *What's happening to me?*

"Oh, Axel. I haven't felt like this in a long time. You make me feel like a woman again."

"I'm glad," he murmured. "You make me feel like a man, Cassie." He captured her mouth again and deepened their kiss. His tongue stroked Cassie's until she was dizzy. Kissing had never felt like this with Benjamin.

Axel slid the rough pads of his fingers under Cassie's top. He smoothed his palms over her breasts, fondling them and teasing her nipples ever so slightly. Cassie's stomach did flip-flops and she felt tension build inside her. Axel whispered in her ear, "This might be wrong, but you're so fucking tempting."

"How can it be wrong when it feels so right?" His touch lit a fire inside her. His voice, husky with passion, fanned the flames. Every square inch of her body was hot for him.

As they kissed, Axel urged her to stand. It felt good to press her body to his. Cassie wrapped her arms around him, pushing her breasts against his chest.

Axel slid his hand under the hem of Cassie's shorts. Cassie expected him to stroke her aching pussy, but his hands came back around her waist. *Doesn't he want me?*

Cassie parted her thighs, and ground herself against him, trapping his hard bulge between them. *Oh, he wants me. He's afraid he'll scare me off.*

"Axel," she whimpered. "Touch me."

He reached down again. This time he pushed

aside her panties and traced her wet folds. He slid his finger inside her and sparks of electricity shot up her spine. Cassie clutched him for support and rocked her hips against his hand. Axel rubbed her clit, sending her racing toward an orgasm. Suddenly, she came undone. "Axel." Her body convulsed against him.

"So beautiful," he whispered.

It was the most intense orgasm Cassie had ever had. She wanted to give Axel the same pleasure. "Now it's your turn."

Cassie reached down and unzipped his jeans, releasing his stiff cock. Axel seemed surprised. She surprised herself. When had she turned into such a sexual creature? But it was what she wanted. What she needed.

Cassie dropped to her knees in front of him. She had never seen an uncircumcised cock before and she stared as he stroked himself, moving the foreskin back and forth over the head.

With her heart pounding, Cassie reached out and took over, wrapping her fingers around his shaft and pulling his foreskin back and forth the way he had done. Drops of cum leaked from the tip, tempting Cassie to take a taste.

She pulled the foreskin back, placed her lips around the head, and moved her tongue in circles. Humming with pleasure, Cassie took him deep, as far as she could. Axel groaned and gripped her hair, directing her movements. Clearly, he was already reaching the point of no return. Urged on by his needy cries, she tightened her grip and sucked harder.

Axel rewarded her with hot spurts of semen. She swallowed every drop, and kept sucking until he pulled her to her feet. Axel looked at her with adoration. They leaned toward each other for a kiss, but just at that moment, Benny let out a cry.

Cassie bit her lip and looked at Axel. "Sorry."

"Don't be sorry. Go to him, Cassie. He needs you."

"We'll talk tomorrow." Cassie gave him one last kiss and went to her son.

* * *

Benjamin Carlton sat in his New York office and cursed at his computer. Damn that woman! He threw a paperweight across the room. It gouged a hole in the wall and fell to the floor. His secretary came running in. "Are you all right?"

"I didn't call you. Get the fuck out."

"I'm sorry, sir." She backed out of the office and shut the door.

"Women!"

At first Benjamin had felt angry when Cassie had taken off with his son, but when he'd cooled down, he'd felt relieved. She'd done him a favor. He had no one to worry about, no one to answer to. His life was his own.

But now he needed to find them. They'd been gone a while and it wasn't easy to pick up her trail. Even the private dick he hired hadn't had any success. Obviously, she'd kept a low profile and stayed away from social media.

If it weren't for that stupid accident, he'd still be searching for them. The accident could have killed his son, but a Good Samaritan saved the boy, and almost got himself killed. The public ate it up. A *Go Fund Me* page had been started online, and donations poured in for the young man. Evidently, he'd used most of them to start a trust fund for Benjamin. Well, Benjamin didn't need another man's money. His biological father could take care of him very nicely.

God, I hate her. I took care of her and the brat, put a roof over their heads and clothes on their backs, and it wasn't good enough for her. I want to make her suffer. She's going to pay for running off and taking my son away from me. She thinks she's made a new life for her and Benjamin, but I can destroy it all in a moment.

Benjamin Carlton studied the photos on his computer. In one, Cassie's face shone with tears as she sat in the street holding Benjamin, Junior in her arms. In another, their white knight lay on the concrete, paramedics checking his pulse.

Benjamin's gaze bored in on them like a hawk studying his prey. Cassie looked beautiful, even with tears streaking her face, but she was a devil in disguise. She deserved everything he intended for her. He would make her beg for mercy, but there would be none.

Chapter Four

They'd grown close, but Cassie knew Axel was still holding part of himself back. She hoped tonight would change that. He'd planned a dinner date just for the two of them and Cassie intended to make the most of it.

Mrs. May had agreed to baby-sit and they would have the alone time they needed so badly, time for a serious conversation and time for other things.

Cassie's desire grew stronger every time she saw Axel. The other night had just been an appetizer. Already, her body felt hot and flushed, just knowing that tonight they'd finish what they started. Cassie wasn't a virgin, but she felt nervous and giddy.

Axel wasn't like Benjamin. He cared about her pleasure, and the anticipation of being with him drove her crazy. Meeting him had changed her life in so many ways. She felt happier than she thought possible.

After the heartache Benjamin had put her through, it was hard to comprehend how she'd fallen so hard for another man, but Axel filled a void in her heart. She vowed not to let bad memories and old fears stop her from living her life. A life she wanted to share with Axel.

* * *

Axel was running late. He glanced at his watch and confirmed their date was in five minutes. A real date. Just the two of them. The kindly Mrs. May had agreed to stay with Benny. It turned out that the old woman was a hopeless romantic who thought Cassie and Axel were perfect for each other. *If she knew the real me, she'd run for the hills.* But it was just a date, nothing serious. *Yeah, keep telling yourself that.*

Axel had made reservations at a fancy restaurant downtown. Normally the place was booked for weeks, but he'd gotten lucky. Someone had canceled just before he called. It would cost him two weeks' salary, but nothing was too good for Cassie.

And after dinner... Well, he tried not to dwell on that. Nature would take its course. Or not. Letting out a deep breath, Axel tried to tamp down his arousal. *Good luck with that.* After a few minutes, he locked his door and walked down the hall to pick up his date.

Mrs. May answered Cassie's door. "Your date's here," she called over her shoulder. "Come in, Axel." Mrs. May lowered her voice an octave. "She's been fussing with her hair for the last thirty minutes."

Embarrassed, Axel took a seat on the couch. He looked around. "Where's Benny?"

"Oh, the little darlin' is already asleep. He's such an --"

"Ax!" Benny's screech cut off the rest of Mrs. May's words. The boy ran out of the bedroom, lunged at Axel, and wrapped his arms around Axel's legs. If Axel didn't know better, he'd think Benny was part wolf cub. Swinging him up toward the ceiling made Benny scream with delight.

Cassie appeared. Distracted, she ran a hand through her hair. "He wouldn't close his eyes until he could say goodnight to you."

"Thanks, buddy," Axel said. "I wanted to see you, too."

Axel looked over at Cassie. Her wide smile showed off her straight white teeth. He remembered how it had felt when those teeth grazed his cock. *Damn, why can't I stop thinking about sex?*

A voice whispered in Axel's head, *"Make love to Cassie. Stop bottling up your urges."*

Axel's wolf was his guiding light. Maybe it was time to start listening to him.

Cassie reached out and touched his arm. "Would you mind tucking Benny in?"

"I'd love to." Axel carried the boy back into the bedroom and sang an old lullaby to him as he tucked him in. He couldn't help it, he felt like Benny was his son. If only. Benny fell asleep and Axel tucked the blanket around him and left the bedroom.

"Sorry about that," Cassie said.

"Don't ever be sorry. Benny comes first. Besides, I needed my Benny fix."

Cassie faked a frown. "Oh? Is that all you need?"

God, she was so sweet, and funny, too. Not to mention she had a nice round ass and a set of tits that made his hands itch. He loved everything about her. Axel winked. "I could use a little more time with his mother."

"I can arrange that."

"I've heard that before. You're all talk, girlfriend."

Cassie looked a little surprised at his comment, but she grabbed his hand and tugged him toward the door. "Come on, Prince Charming. We'll be late for dinner."

Axel drove. He parked in a garage and they walked around the corner to the fancy restaurant he'd selected. It was one of the most expensive in Philadelphia, but it was worth it to hear Cassie ooh and ah over the large, elegant dining room. There were crystal chandeliers and the tables were dressed with fine linen and fresh flowers.

After they were seated, a waiter appeared to take their drink order. Axel would have liked a cocktail to calm his nerves, but he was driving so he ordered sparkling water. Cassie joined him and they toasted their friendship.

The waiters were attentive without being overbearing. The filets were delicious and cooked to perfection.

Cassie and Axel made small talk about Benny and work. By the time the waiter arrived with dessert, slices of decadent red velvet cheesecake, the small talk had become awkward.

Cassie steered the conversation toward Axel's family. He deftly changed the subject by asking about Benny's father.

Cassie shrugged. "He's not in the picture."

Axel wanted to hear the truth about Benny's father, but he didn't want to upset Cassie. It was completely frustrating but he dropped the subject because he didn't want to ruin Cassie's night. Besides, he wanted a little more alone time with Cassie. "How about a nightcap at my place?"

"I thought you'd never ask."

* * *

Cassie hoped she hadn't upset Axel by not being more forthcoming. She trusted him, but if he inadvertently let something slip, it could mean trouble for her and Benny. On the short drive back, she kept up a steady chatter about their fantastic dinner.

Once they were inside Axel's apartment, Cassie reached for her phone. Not wanting to pop in and wake Benny, Cassie opted to call Mrs. May for an update.

"Is everything okay?" Axel asked.

"Yes. He's sound asleep. Mrs. May couldn't stop raving about him. I'm afraid she might steal him away from me."

"She'd make a great grandmother."

For a moment, Cassie felt sad that Benny couldn't see his real grandparents. Then she brushed it aside. They'd never been interested in him since the day he was born. It didn't seem like they cared about their own son.

Then Axel took her in his arms and wiped away her melancholy thoughts. He captured her lips in a kiss that set her heart pounding. When his mouth crushed hers, sparks exploded behind her eyelids. Axel slid his tongue along the seam of Cassie's lips and she opened for him. She'd give him anything he wanted. Cassie moaned when Axel slipped his tongue between her lips.

Axel gently explored Cassie's shoulders and back. Even through her dress, Axel's touch sent her spiraling out of control. *I want to feel those hands on my bare skin.*

Cassie rubbed her hips against his. His erection felt as big and hard as a baseball bat. Filled with raw hunger, Cassie moaned. "Axel?"

"I'm here, baby."

"I need you."

"Are you sure, Cassie?"

"God, yes. I want you."

To show him how much, Cassie unzipped his slacks and pulled them down over his hips.

Axel kicked them aside and removed his shirt. "Now it's your turn, gorgeous."

He watched intently as Cassie removed her clothes. Finally, she stood in front of him in her panties. He hooked his fingers in the waistband and pushed them down. "You're so beautiful. I want you so much."

Axel's voice was filled with so much emotion, it stirred Cassie's heart. She wanted him, too. She wrapped her fingers around his cock and stroked its length, enjoying the silky, smooth feel of his hot flesh.

Axel's hands tangled in her long hair "Oh, God, baby. That feels so good."

Axel's moan was music to her ears. Wanting to hear more, she started to pump his shaft harder. Axel's breathing quickened. He sucked on his finger and then reached down between Cassie's thighs, rubbing her sensitive clit with light teasing touches. She started moaning and rocking her hips against his hand. Her excitement boiled higher and she wondered if they would make it to the bed.

"You're so responsive, so wet and hot," he murmured. "I want to be inside you."

"I want that, too. Fuck me, Axel."

He picked her up and carried her to his bed, laid her on it, and straddled her body. He looked down at her, silent for a moment. Cassie worried that he was having second thoughts. "Axel?"

His lower lip trembled and he bit it.

"What's wrong?"

"I don't have a condom."

"I haven't had sex in a long time, but I started taking birth control pills."

There was an embarrassing pause, then Axel swallowed and spoke nervously. "I've never had sex. I'm afraid I'll hurt you."

Cassie was surprised, but happy, too. "I'm glad I'm your first. I wish I could give you that, but it's too late. I've been in a bad relationship and I've had a baby." Cassie kissed him reassuringly. "You won't hurt me."

"Don't be sorry. That bad relationship produced something wonderful. Benny."

"You're right." Cassie captured his lips with a

deep, emotional kiss.

Axel whispered in her ear. "Uh… Can you do something for me, Cassie?"

"Anything."

"Would you get on all fours?"

Cassie was a little put-off. She really wanted to see Axel's face as they made love, but she realized he might be shy. Besides, she hungered for him too much to refuse. Her vagina throbbed and she ached to be filled.

Gone was the meek little waitress. Axel made her feel naughty and sexy. She could handle doggy style. She rolled over and lay on her stomach.

Axel growled. "Lift your ass, baby."

Cassie burned with embarrassment, but the heat of arousal surpassed her shame. She got on her knees and elbows, offering herself to him.

Axel caressed her ass. "I wish you could see how beautiful you look." He leaned over her and whispered, "This isn't just a quick fuck for me, Cassie. I care about you. I want to make love to you."

Cassie swallowed the lump in her throat. Maybe it was just wishful thinking, but she believed that what they had together was real. "Oh, Axel. I feel the same."

He reached around her and played with her sensitive nub, then pushed two fingers inside her. "You're so wet, baby. Are you ready for more?"

Cassie whimpered softly and pushed against his hand. "Yes. Oh, yes."

Cassie felt the broad head of his cock nudge her opening. As wet as she was, there was still pain, but she arched her back to give him a better angle. Axel put a hand on her back to steady her and pushed inside slow and easy. A moan escaped Cassie's lips as she gave in to his possession. She gripped the sheets.

"Oh, God. Oh, God."

Axel froze. "Are you okay?"

In response, Cassie pushed back, seating Axel deep inside her. "I love having your big cock inside me. Don't stop."

He growled with pleasure. "You feel amazing. I love your tight heat squeezing my cock."

Axel withdrew partway, and in slow, controlled movements filled her again. Cassie wanted more. She couldn't help shoving her hips back against him.

"Relax, baby. I'm going to give you what you want." Axel began thrusting in earnest and they groaned in unison.

Axel rode her with a strong rhythm while she squirmed beneath him. He might have been a virgin, but he seemed to know exactly what Cassie needed, varying his thrusts with a combination of strength and tenderness. Their scents mingled and filled the room with a wild, musky aroma. Their incoherent sounds and ragged breathing echoed around them. Cassie wanted to make this lovemaking last as long as possible. She struggled to hold off her climax, but her pleasure grew too intense.

Axel reached around and teased Cassie's clit, making her even hotter. Sensation coursed through her body and she begged for release. "Please, please, please..."

Axel murmured soothing words against her heated skin. He kissed a sensitive spot on Cassie's neck. Suddenly, he closed his mouth over that spot and his teeth pierced Cassie's flesh. She screamed as sparks raced from the wound throughout her body. Axel licked the bite, and any pain was replaced by pleasure. Suddenly, he pulled her back, driving deep inside her. Cassie's pussy contracted, squeezing Axel's hard flesh, and she came like never before. Her spasms milked a climax from Axel. He let out a low growl and emptied himself inside her.

* * *

Axel sprawled atop Cassie, boneless, sated, and relieved. For a moment, he'd had trouble pulling out. Terrified, he thought that the muscles in Cassie's vagina had tightened around his wolf's knot and they were locked together like two fornicating dogs. A more experienced shifter would have thought of that. All it took was a few deep, calming breaths and he slid out of Cassie's tight sheath. Did that mean they couldn't have children together? He had no idea. It didn't matter. They had Benny, and they could adopt. Perhaps that would be a better alternative for a shifter and a human. Oh, my God. He knew so little about her, and yet he was already thinking marriage.

Cassie squirmed under him.

"I'm sorry, baby. I didn't mean to suffocate you." He rolled them to their sides, so her back was to his chest. "You okay?"

"Yes. You're a wonderful lover." Cassie cuddled against him, her body slick with perspiration.

Mine. Emotion swept over Axel. He felt fiercely possessive and he was pretty damn sure he was crazy in love with Cassie Miller.

* * *

Cassie opened her eyes, and for a moment she didn't know where she was. Then she realized she was in Axel's bed. Still more asleep than awake, Cassie didn't want to move. It felt good to lie there wrapped in Axel's warm embrace. She felt as if she belonged there with him, as if they were made for each other. This sense of belonging was new, a feeling she'd never experienced with Benjamin. She could get used to it.

They were naked under the sheets, and Cassie loved the feel of Axel's skin against hers. Axel's warm breath fanned her shoulder and his arm was heavy around her waist. She felt safe and protected.

Gently, she extricated herself and turned to look at the man beside her. She traced the planes of his face, memorizing his features. She watched the rise and fall of his chest as he slept. *What are you dreaming about? I hope it's me.*

If only this could last forever and they could be a real family. But that would mean telling Axel about her past, and subjecting him to a life of hiding from her abusive ex. What man would want a woman with so much baggage?

Cassie pushed aside the depressing thoughts. She wanted to enjoy the moment. Those thoughts would claim her again soon enough. They always did. When she least expected it, Benjamin's face would appear to her, reminding her that he was still out there somewhere, and could come back at any time. But for now, she felt safe from the memories that had almost destroyed her.

Tonight, she'd felt closer to Axel than ever before. It was more than friendship, more than fucking, and it shook her to her core. When she looked at Axel, she knew she didn't want to be with anyone else in the world. It was love, and it scared her. She'd thought she'd felt it once before, but it had taken her on a path that had almost destroyed her.

That was different. She refused to let it intrude on this time with Axel. Cassie was utterly content to lie with him forever. Until her gaze landed on the alarm clock across the room. 3 A.M.

Oh my God. Benny!

And poor Mrs. May. She left Axel's bed and

dressed quietly.

* * *

Cassie had her key out, ready to unlock her front door, but it was already open. A dreadful churning started in her stomach.

There were no lights on in the apartment, another bad omen. Cassie flicked the switch, and blinked as light flooded the living room. She'd expected to find Mrs. May asleep on the couch, but the room was empty.

Perhaps she'd fallen asleep in the bedroom. Cassie opened the door. By the light coming in from the living room, she could see Mrs. May lying face down on the floor.

Cassie's heart dropped as she crouched beside the old woman and checked for a pulse. Tears streamed down her face when she couldn't find one. At first, she thought heart attack, then she saw the purple bruises around Mrs. May's throat. *Oh my God! She's been murdered.*

Shocked and frightened, Cassie ran over to the crib. It was empty.

She picked up the pile of blankets and buried her face in them, smelling Benny's sweet baby scent. Seeing that he was gone completely broke her. Cassie let out a keening wail and started trembling uncontrollably. Her worst nightmare had come to pass. This had to be Benjamin's doing.

Shock, panic, horror, helplessness… Emotions bombarded Cassie. And on top of it all, came the guilt. She blamed herself for not being there when they needed her. Instead, she'd been lost in her own pleasure. She wanted to curl up next to Mrs. May and die too. But that wouldn't help Benny. She couldn't let that monster have him. For the first time she noticed a handwritten note that had been left in the crib.

I have the boy. If you want to see him again, do exactly as I say.

Don't call the police. Don't tell anyone.
Come to the Hub Motel, Route 1, Room 101
Destroy this note.

Cassie would do as it said. What choice did she have? She knew he meant it. If she didn't follow his instructions, she'd never see Benny again. She'd known this would happen one day. She should have been more careful. She had never felt so alone, but she had to bring her baby home.

Forcing aside her fear, she slipped the note and a small knife into her handbag and left the apartment.

* * *

Axel woke and stretched with drowsy pleasure. His morning wood gave him a standing ovation and he turned over, eager to fuck Cassie again. He reached out, disappointed when he found the bed cold and empty. He'd slept longer than he'd realized. It was already 6:45. Who knew that sex before bed would give him such a good night's sleep?

He'd never gotten to third base back home and last night, he'd felt like a horny inexperienced teenager, but Cassie had cast a spell over him. They were two different species, yet they'd come together as one. Instinctively, he'd known how to please her. Well, maybe his wolf had helped. There was something to be said for animal instinct. He wished Cassie could have stuck around, and not just for sex. Axel craved her company, but Benny came first. He was an early riser and would be missing his mommy.

I'll go to her. Coffee and bagels coming up.

While the coffee perked, Axel jumped in the shower.

Chapter Five

Cassie could hear Benny crying through the motel room door. She pounded on it, even gave it a kick. "Open up."

Benjamin opened the door and she pushed past him. Benny was sitting on the bed crying. "Benny. Mommy's here, baby."

Benny reached out his arms. His face was red and streaked with tears. "Mommy, Mommy, Mommy."

Cassie grabbed him up and held him close. "I've got you, peanut." Her eyes filled with tears as she looked over at Benjamin. "How could you? You're a monster."

"You took my son away, so who's the real monster?"

"You never wanted him."

Benjamin shrugged. "I changed my mind."

"I don't believe you. Why now?"

"I guess it wouldn't hurt to tell you." Benjamin spoke with unconcealed contempt. "As you know, I'm an only child, the last male of my family, and the only one who will be able to keep our name alive. My father is a rich man, the owner of a large corporation, and well known in the community. He wants to avoid embarrassment and keep our legacy alive."

"You think my son is an embarrassment?"

"Only if he turns up later and tries to gain control of the business. My father wants to raise him as a true Carlton, a man worthy to carry on our name and run the business someday."

"No way. I'll never marry you and we don't want any part of your business."

Benjamin laughed, a humorless vicious sound.

"Who said anything about marriage? I wouldn't marry you before, and I certainly wouldn't marry you now. You think I want a dumb little waitress running my house and raising my kid?"

"He's mine," Cassie shouted. "I gave birth to him without you, and I was always there for him. When he was sad, upset, or sick, I was the one who took care of him. I won't let you to take him away from me." She moved toward the door. "We're leaving."

"Sit down!"

Cassie froze. The authority and anger in his voice frightened her, but it made her more anxious to get away. She ran to the door and turned the knob. Locked. She threw herself against it. "Let us out."

"Sit down, Cassie. We're playing by my rules now." Benjamin shoved a bottle at her. "Feed him so we can talk."

Crying, Cassie sat on the bed and offered the bottle to Benny. Her ex was an inhuman monster. It was hard to believe they were even the same species. She should have called the police, but it was too late now. Maybe if she talked to him, she could stall this and think of a way out. She remembered the knife in her purse. "Raising a child is a lifetime commitment. Your parents are too old, and I know you don't want the responsibility."

"You're right on both counts. Benjamin will go to a good boarding school. It'll make a real man out of him."

Cassie scoffed. "Like you?"

"Exactly. I can do much more for him than you can. He'll have a good life, everything money can buy."

"A child needs more than money. He needs love."

"Love is a foolish, fleeting emotion, while money can buy anything -- clothes, travel, the best medical care, even love."

"You're wrong and I'll never stand by and let you ruin Benny's life."

"Of course you won't." He looked at her sadly. "Poor Benjamin, he was so young when his mother died."

Cassie's blood turned ice cold. "You wouldn't?"

"Oh, but I would. I'm going to do it for Benjamin."

Cassie looked down at the baby. His breathing was shallow and he lay limply in her arms. "What's wrong with him?"

"He'll be fine. I put a few drops of something in his bottle to make him sleepy. I saved the rest for you."

"You're crazy. You'll never get away with this."

"Like I said, money can buy anything, even a good alibi."

Cassie squeezed her eyes shut and said a prayer. *Please, God, save my baby.*

* * *

Axel's heart ached. He sat on the floor cradling Mrs. May's lifeless body. He'd grown so fond of her in the short time he'd known her. And Cassie and Benny... Where were they? This was a nightmare. A nightmare that was all his fault. Deep down he'd known Cassie was running from something or someone. He should have questioned her, been more protective.

You're here now. Do something.

What?

You're a wolf, aren't you? Act like one. Or let me out.

Axel shook his head. *No, no, no.* He didn't dare shift among the humans. Someone might shoot him.

And if he did find Cassie, she'd know what he really was.

That didn't matter now. Cassie and Benny were in danger and only he could save them. The police would never find Cassie as quickly as he could. There was no time to lose.

Preparing to shift, Axel undressed and set his clothes aside. He closed his eyes, rotated his shoulders in a forward direction, and then rotated them backwards, to loosen up his muscles. He shook his arms and hands, trying to get out all the kinks. It had been a long time since he shifted.

His human body had hundreds of muscles, and they all responded to signals from his brain. Axel's brain went to work. He pictured his wolf and let his brain-muscle interaction do the rest. His muscles stretched and contracted under his flesh. When he was a kid, he would scream with the pain, but over the years his muscles had developed a molecular memory of the process and now they morphed with ease.

The beast inside Axel fought to get out, anxious to find its mate. His spine bent, forcing him to his hands and knees. His palms changed to pads. Brown fur spread over his body. His face grew longer, and sharp fangs broke through his gums. The pressure at the base of his spine was relieved with the emergence of a bushy tail.

It felt good to be in wolf skin. He'd missed this part of himself. He was more than human, he was a shifter, and he needed to nurture his wolf spirit. If he got out of this alive, he'd let his wolf out more often.

Axel had burned a hell of a lot of adrenaline to crack his bones and stretch his muscles, but he had plenty of energy left for the task at hand. Panting softly, he padded around the apartment, imprinting

Cassie's and Benny's scents on his brain. He scented the kidnapper, and a growl came from his chest.

He'd left the apartment door ajar, and now he slipped through it and moved down the hall toward his destination. For once, he was glad he wasn't as big as the others in his pack. He'd fit down the trash chute with no problem. What he lacked in size, he made up for with his sense of smell. Axel was one hell of a tracker, and he couldn't wait to get on the trail. But first he had to get out of the building. He used his long claws to open the door, so he could jump into the chute. Down he slid, finally landing in the dumpster outside.

Axel leaped out and shook himself off. He picked up two trails. One led to Cassie's empty parking spot, the other to where a strange car had been parked. *Damn you, Cassie. Why didn't you call me instead of taking off after this creep alone?* Hopefully, both trails would lead him to the same place.

Cars were harder to follow than prey that traveled on foot, but not impossible. Axel's prey drive kicked in -- search, stalk, chase, kill. His nose in the wind, he went on the hunt. He was made for this.

Axel's nose led him to an old motel not far outside East Falls. Cassie's old Toyota, parked outside Room 101, was proof positive. He'd found his prey. Now to attract their attention and get inside the room.

Axel scratched at the door, but no one opened it. Stronger measures were needed. He threw himself at the door again and again. Finally, he heard someone fooling with the lock.

The door opened and Axel's hackles rose. He snarled at the man blocking his way.

"What's this? Do you have a dog, Cassie?"

Axel spotted Cassie behind the man and he

slipped past him. Benny was lying on a bed, out cold. Axel growled and leaped onto the bed. He sniffed Benny's face to see if he was breathing. Son of a bitch. The boy had been drugged. Axel could smell it on him.

Cassie screamed and came at Axel with a knife in her hand. "Get away from my baby."

How could Axel let her know he meant no harm to her or Benny? Maybe a whimper and a lick? He turned his muzzle, but he found himself staring at the barrel of a gun. Axel snarled and showed his fangs.

Cassie ran at the kidnapper. "No. Don't shoot. You might hit Benny."

The man shoved her away. Cassie fell to the floor and hit her head on the side of the dresser.

"It looks like you saved me the job of killing her, doggy."

Axel was a peaceful man but something snapped inside him and his wolf turned into a raging beast. His powerful hind legs propelled him off the bed and he lunged at his prey. Two big paws hit the kidnapper's chest and knocked him backwards. He landed on his ass, and the gun flew out of his hand.

Axel followed him to the floor. He straddled his prey and bared his teeth, taking great satisfaction in the man's frightened expression. There was no stopping now. Axel locked his powerful jaws around the man's neck and crushed his windpipe. He didn't let go until he was sure his prey had no more life in him. Panting, he stared at the dead man, sickened by the sight of his torn throat. He'd had no choice.

Cassie was unconscious, but still alive. Axel weighed his options. He could do a runner, and Cassie would never know he'd been there, or he could stay and take care of them. His wolf urged him to act like a man. Right again. Axel prepared to shift back to his human form.

He was still crouched by the body when a touch on his shoulder made him jump. Seeing Cassie standing over him, he steeled himself for the fear she must be feeling.

"Axel, your dog saved my life." There was a hint of admiration in her voice. "Well, you and the dog. Where did he go? How did you find us? Where are your clothes?" She stopped short. "Sorry."

Axel had a way out, but he wouldn't take it. It was time to tell Cassie the truth. "Don't be sorry. You deserve answers to your questions. It was me, Cassie. I'm the dog you saw." He couldn't look at Cassie for fear of seeing horror and disgust on her face.

"What are you talking about?"

Axel moved away when Cassie tried to touch him again. "Do you remember, I told you I heal fast? Well, that's not all I can do. I'm a shifter, Cassie. A wolf-shifter. That was me you saw, in my wolf skin."

Cassie's eyes went wide. "I didn't believe shifters were real. Why didn't you tell me?"

"Why didn't you tell me you were running from a lunatic?"

"At first I didn't trust you, and then I was afraid to involve you."

Axel smiled sadly. "And I was afraid you'd hate me."

"I could never hate you. I'll tell you everything, but we need to get Benny out of here. He gave him something, a drug."

"That bastard. Take Benny to the hospital. Get him checked out. Don't leave anything of yours here. All the evidence will say this man was attacked by a dog. You'll be out of it."

"What about you?"

"I'll travel on all fours. Go. Take care of Benny."

* * *

It was night when Cassie got home from the hospital. She saw police tape covering her apartment door and went straight to Axel's apartment.

He opened the door and took Benny from her.

"How is he?"

Benny threw his arms around Axel. "I okay."

Axel let out a sigh of relief. "You sure are, buddy."

"He's a trooper," Cassie said. "I told them Benny got into my sleeping meds and they ran tests on him. He didn't have enough drugs in him to cause any lasting effects and they let him sleep it off. I was afraid they'd call child protection on me, but the doctor remembered me. He gave me a long lecture and told me to lock up my drugs. Anyway, Benny is fine. Thanks to you."

"I'm just glad I got there in time." There was an awkward silence. "The police were in your apartment when I got back. Someone must have seen the open door. They questioned everyone, including me. I told them that you and Benny spent the night here, before you took him to the hospital. They think we're having an affair. I hope you don't mind."

Cassie blinked back tears. *Is that what he thinks? An affair? I thought we meant more to each other.*

"You can't go in your apartment. It's a crime scene. You and Benny can stay here. I'll be leaving in the morning. This apartment is yours as long as you need it."

"You're going to leave us?"

"It's for the best. You and Benny will be safe now. You don't have to be afraid anymore."

"I'm afraid to lose you, Axel."

"Cassie, did you hear what I told you at the motel?"

"So?"

"I'm not like you."

"The important thing is that you're not like my ex. You're a kind, loving person. If I didn't believe that, I wouldn't have let you touch me."

"But you didn't know who you were getting involved with."

"And now I do."

"You're not thinking clearly, Cassie. You'll grow to hate me."

"Do you hate me for being human?"

"Of course not. I love you."

"Love you," Benny piped up.

Axel smiled at him. "And I couldn't love you more if you were my biological cub. Er, I mean my son. But shifters are forbidden to be with humans."

"Then why me? Why didn't you choose another shifter for your first?"

Axel couldn't meet her eyes. "Because my wolf led me to you. The beast wants what it wants."

She stopped breathing for a heartbeat, then asked in a whisper, "And the man. What does he want?"

Axel burst out desperately, "You!"

Cassie's heart took a leap. "Then what's the problem?"

"You don't understand."

"Then explain, please."

Axel's tortured gaze made her heart ache. He let out a groan. "We claimed you with our bite. I already feel like you're mine. Ours. Shifters mate for life."

"Admit it. You won't be able to live without me."

A melancholy frown flitted across Axel's features. "It will be hard, but I can't force you into being my mate. It's a strong commitment for a human woman who doesn't know what she's getting into."

"I know I can't lose you. The most important thing is that we can shed our masks and be honest with each other. To hell with the rest of the world. If they can't accept us, that's their problem."

"Are you sure?"

"I always wanted a dog."

Axel threw back his head and laughed. The sound was music to Cassie's ears.

"And a real family, one that laughs together. I want that, too."

"You make me happy." Axel leaned in for a kiss, but Benny's head popped up and intercepted it. They both kissed him, then each other.

"So what happens now?" Cassie asked.

"Now, we let go of the past, wipe out the fears that ruled us, and start a new chapter."

Gale Stanley

Gale Stanley grew up in Philadelphia, PA. She was the kid who always had her nose in a book, her head in the clouds, and her hands on a pad and pencil.

Some things never change.

Gale at Changeling: changelingpress.com/gale-stanley-a-199

Changeling Press E-Books

More Sci-Fi, Fantasy, Paranormal, and BDSM adventures available in e-book format for immediate download at ChangelingPress.com -- Werewolves, Vampires, Dragons, Shapeshifters and more -- Erotic Tales from the edge of your imagination.

What are E-Books?

E-books, or electronic books, are books designed to be read in digital format -- on your desktop or laptop computer, notebook, tablet, Smart Phone, or any electronic e-book reader.

Where can I get Changeling Press E-Books?

Changeling Press e-books are available at ChangelingPress.com, Amazon, Apple Books, Barnes & Noble, and Kobo/Walmart.

Changeling Press.LLC

ChangelingPress.com

www.ingramcontent.com/pod-product-compliance
Lightning Source LLC
Chambersburg PA
CBHW070015260626
47159CB00005B/1815